Jake took a deep breath and made a rush for the trees. He got halfway when a rifle barked. Something stung his left foot, but he managed to stumble on to the trees. Once there, he swung the Sharps back toward the camp. When the sandy-haired teen emerged from cover long enough, Jake fired. His shot shattered the Bluejacket's rifle. Eddie fired as well, shattering the fellow's collarbone. Gene killed the man with a clean shot through the left eye.

"I give up!" the last of the thieves cried, waving a white kerchief.

"Keep down, boy!" Lofland shouted as Judson jumped out.

The outlaw pulled a well-concealed pistol and fired.

THE
SHAWNEE
TRAIL

G. Clifton Wisler

FAWCETT GOLD MEDAL • NEW YORK

A Fawcett Gold Medal Book
Published by Ballantine Books
Copyright © 1993 by G. Clifton Wisler

Library of Congress Catalog Card Number: 93-90200

ISBN 0-449-14831-9

Manufactured in the United States of America

First Edition: September 1993

1

Jake Wetherby doffed his broad-brimmed hat and mopped the sweat on his forehead with a kerchief. It had turned hot—even for Texas. May had a way of doing that. You could expect a mild spell, but you were generally disappointed. Texas was prone to extremes. Flood and drought.

Jake spit the sour taste from his mouth and slid off his horse.

"You feel it, too, don't you, Maizy girl?" he asked, stroking the speckled mare's flank.

The horse stomped its feet and gave a slight shudder.

"Just the wind," Jake muttered. He left Maizy beside Spring Creek, knowing the mare would be content to remain there, satisfying her thirst. Hobbles would be a waste of time. Jake, meanwhile, turned and started toward a nearby hill. There, standing side by side in a sea of Indian paintbrushes, were the two stone markers he'd hauled out from Dallas. He and his brothers hadn't managed anything so fine originally, and winter had a way of weathering boards. The stones would last.

"Ma, Pa," he whispered as he knelt beside the stones. "It's fitting you have something permanent. People ought to know you came this way."

Yes, they had been the settling type. The peach orchard and the neatly plowed fields proved that. The house and barn had given way to Texas lightning. Fire had no respect for a man's efforts.

Jake scowled as he remembered fighting that fire, trying

to save some remnant of better days. It had been hopeless, though. It always was.

"Can't hold on to anything very long," he grumbled.

Well, he was past trying now. Jake Wetherby would leave no stone markers on the land to mark his passing. No, he wasn't much more than a gust of wind blowing across the Llano. No one took much notice of him. Nor was there any need.

"Don't fret over it, Ma," he said, laughing as he thought back to her countless efforts to educate him. "You never expected me to get myself elected governor. Haven't been hung yet. I've got near a hundred dollars cash money to my name, and I own three good horses."

Jake couldn't help telling himself that was more than his father had managed. When Joe Wetherby died, he'd left mostly debts to his sons. They hadn't even had a roof over their heads. Jake's youthful stepmother had taken young Joe into Harrison's Crossroads. Frank Selwyn had taken in the other three boys. Jake, well, he'd gone his own way, like always.

That seemed like a long time ago now. It wasn't. It still grieved Jake that he hadn't been able to provide for his young brothers, but that was about to change. That summer they'd be together again. Yes, sir, the Wetherbys were about to ride north.

"I got to admit, Ma, Miz Selwyn's done right by the boys," Jake confessed. "Keeps their shirts mended, and even Josh's taking on some weight. They get out to meetings whenever the preacher comes, and they do their lessons. Better'n me, I expect. Before she wrings all the sass out of 'em, though, I'll take 'em up north. Nothing like an adventure to open your eyes to the world's possibilities."

Jake nodded to himself. That last phrase had been one of his grandpa's favorites. Possibilities. Wasn't that all a man could expect out of life? It was up to him to do something with them.

Maizy stirred restlessly, and Jake slowly rose.

"I know, girl," he said, eyeing the mare. "Wouldn't do

to be late. You don't get invited to Sunday dinner every week.''

He frowned a final farewell and briefly touched the rough surface of the gravestones. Then he turned and hurried to his horse. He climbed atop Maizy with the sort of effortless ease only a man accustomed to long hours of riding could manage. Then, with a slight movement of his knees, he nudged Maizy into a trot.

The Selwyn farm was only a mile or so downstream from the old Wetherby place. The whole property belonged to Frank Selwyn now, but old-timers continued to refer to the land's previous owner. That confused occasional newcomers, who often failed to understand why three Wetherby orphans lived with the Selwyns if they had land of their own.

"Half of 'em wonder about it," Jake's seventeen-year-old brother Jericho noted. "Other half think we're all Frank's boys."

"Well, he does take in strays, doesn't he?" Jake had asked.

Besides Jake's brothers, Frank Selwyn had his wife Rebecca's rogue brother Silas Garrett living there.

"I don't suppose Frank minded much before, when there was all that land to clear," Jericho had observed the year before. "Now the Selwyns have got their own four youngsters, the house is getting downright crowded."

Jake agreed. It was why he had finally accepted Rebecca Selwyn's dinner invitation. It was time he took charge of his brothers again. Time he relieved those good people of their extra burden.

When Jake arrived at the Selwyn place, he found Jericho waiting.

"Not late, am I, Jer?" Jake asked as he dismounted.

"Not for dinner," Jericho answered. "Thought you might come a hair early so we could have a proper visit."

Jake started to explain, but he swallowed the unspoken words. Surprises were best shared at the proper moment. No good spoiling it beforehand.

"I'll say one thing," Jericho observed as he took charge

of Maizy. "You prettied yourself up. No girls here to impress, you know."

"Thought it best if I didn't smell like horses," Jake explained. "You might not mind me that way, but Miz Selwyn just might invite me to take my meal out to the barn."

"She's got boys of her own, and three of us Wetherbys," Jericho declared. "Not to mention Si! She's used to boys and their antics."

"I suppose. Still, never hurts to make yourself a hair more presentable."

"I thought you been out on the plain all spring," Jericho grumbled. "Sounds like you've gone and gotten civilized!"

"Not altogether," Jake said, taking off his hat and shaking the hair out of his eyes.

"I see you put Grandpa's old razor to use," Jericho remarked.

"You used its twin, too," Jake replied. "Won't be too long before you need it regular."

"Be out chasing horses with you by then. No need to shave for the ponies' sake."

"Now there's a truth," Jake agreed. He took a deep breath and gazed soberly at his brother. "Figure you're ready for a real adventure, Jer?"

"I was ready last summer," Jericho declared. "If it wasn't for Jordy and Josh still being so little . . ."

"Guess they're big enough to see to themselves now, huh?"

"Truth is, we all three of us figured we might join you on a horse hunt," Jericho explained. "Si, too."

Jake paused a moment. It was what he wanted to hear, but he didn't want to give himself away. Finally he forced a frown onto his face.

"I don't aim to waste a summer chasing ponies," he said sourly.

Jericho's smile faded. It tore at Jake, seeing Jer lose heart like that. A boy could get to where he'd been disappointed so often he quit hoping for things. The frown would pass, too, though. Jake knew it would.

Jake rested his hat on a peg over the door and followed Jericho through the front of the house and back to the dining room. Jordy and Josh were carrying spare chairs in to the table. Rebecca Selwyn was tending her three smallest boys. Willie, at eight the oldest by four years, was helping Silas Garrett set out plates.

"Jake!" Josh exclaimed, abandoning his chair as he rushed to his older brother's side.

"Howdy, Peanut," Jake said, lifting the boy up onto one shoulder. It wasn't as easy now. Josh was closing in on thirteen, and his eyes had lost some of their old hollow, sickly gaze. His hair was still yellow-white, but there was more color to his flesh.

"You can help with the chairs, Jake," Jordy scolded from the far side of the table.

Jake held onto little Josh a moment longer before returning the youngster to earth.

"You're company," Josh insisted when Jake started toward the kitchen. "It's our chore. We'll do it."

"Sure, Peanut," Jake said, retreating.

"He's growing up," Frank Selwyn observed as he offered Jake his hand.

"They'll go and do that on you," Jake noted as he gripped his host's hand.

Soon all the chairs were in place, and Rebecca Selwyn nodded she was satisfied. Jericho motioned Jake toward a chair at the far end. Jordy sat at one elbow, and Josh climbed into the chair on the other side.

"Let us pray," Selwyn said, bowing his head. The others did likewise, and he spoke a few brief words of thanksgiving before whispering, "Amen."

"Amen," the others echoed.

Platters of food then began making their way around the table. Roast pork, baked potatoes, and cornbread, topped off by greens and stewed plums. Jake ate and ate. He couldn't remember tasting anything half that delicious in ages.

"Sometimes I feel like I'm raising a family of hogs," Rebecca observed.

"Just growing boys's all," Si argued. "You wouldn't want to raise a batch of midgets, would you?"

"Little chance of that," Jake noted. "Even Willie here's stretching himself."

"Has some time before he'll pester me about chasing range ponies," Selwyn noted between bites of potato. "Colonel Duncan keeping you busy, Jake?"

"Middling," Jake answered. "Colonel stays occupied, making plans and all. Dreaming up new schemes to make money."

"Any of it make its way into your pocket?"

"Some," Jake confessed. "Put a little by against future need. Got myself another horse, too."

"You already had two," Josh complained. "Can't ride but one at a time."

"Oh, that's true enough," Jake admitted. "If all you need to do's go into town once a week or carry yourself to school. But a cowboy needs fresh mounts."

"A what?" Jericho asked, eyeing Jake suspiciously.

"Cowboy," Jake explained. "Oh, what we used to call a drover. Only these days, it's a man on horse drives the stock."

"Drives 'em where?" Jordy asked, setting down his fork a moment.

"Up north," Jake explained. "Chicago. St. Louis. Wherever the buyers are. Most outfits head for Sedalia, Missouri."

"Up the Shawnee Trail, huh?" Selwyn asked. "That's what the colonel's got on his mind, is it?"

"Others have done it," Jake replied. "Man or two's made a fortune selling his cows up there. Quick profit."

"One or two's made himself some money up there," Selwyn noted. "Others have found mostly trouble. Not much law in the Nations. Tribes demand tolls for crossing their land. You have rivers to cross and storms to survive. Thieves plague that border country, not to mention the trouble you can find in Missouri."

"Colonel Duncan's got himself a man to deal with all

that,'' Jake explained. ''Stan Lofland. Was a Texas Ranger for a time. Sheriff down south, too.''

''I've heard of him,'' Selwyn muttered. ''Paid killer. But maybe that's what you need to travel that country. I suppose he's got a big outfit, the colonel.''

''Plans on fifteen, twenty hands,'' Jake said, sighing. ''Has most hired on already, but he asked me to ask around. I told him I knew of some good hands eager to find themselves an adventure.''

''Jake?'' Jericho asked, staring hard at his older brother.

''You can't mean your brothers,'' Rebecca objected. ''They have school.''

''It's mostly over, ma'am,'' Jake argued. ''I don't figure there's much more that old woman can teach Jer anyhow.''

''If he's going, so am I!'' Jordy insisted.

''Me, too,'' Josh piped in.

''I'd be more help'n any of them,'' Si argued. ''I'm older, too. Eighteen.''

''You'd be welcome, Si,'' Jake replied, ''but you best discuss your responsibilities with Frank. He might need help with his crop.''

''And us?'' Jericho asked.

''Was you three I came to ask,'' Jake explained.

''They're too young,'' Rebecca insisted. ''Especially Jordan and Joshua.''

''They've been through harder trials than any they'll find on the Shawnee Trail,'' Jake argued. ''What's more, we haven't had much time together, the four of us. I figure we owe ourselves this summer to get reacquainted.''

''You'd be welcome to join us here, Jacob Henry,'' Rebecca said, breathing deeply. ''But to take those boys out—''

''Jer's as old now as I was when Pa died,'' Jake noted. ''Jordy's near fifteen. Josh may be small, but he'll have three brothers looking out after him.''

''You said yourself I was growing tall,'' Josh declared, gazing on the woman with pleading eyes.

''I don't know about this,'' Selwyn grumbled.

"Sir, the country's changing," Jake said, dabbing at his chin with a napkin. "Who knows how long a man can chase down mavericks on the open range? Markets can turn sour, too. Next summer they may not want Texas beef up north. Just now there's money to be made trailing cattle. What's more, it's as close to a real adventure as we're apt to come across. We've got no Mexican army to fight."

"You went off to war at seventeen, Frank," Si said, gazing pleadingly at his brother-in-law.

"War's a different thing altogether," Selwyn argued. "No one's aiming to burn down your home if you shy away from this cattle drive."

"It's too perilous an undertaking," Rebecca complained. "You'll get yourselves killed."

"I won't say it doesn't have its dangers, ma'am," Jake replied. "You won't find a real adventure that doesn't. You know the colonel, though. He's no man to take undue chances. I'll be there, watching out for my brothers like I always have. We need this time, the four of us. Life's sort of short-changed us the past three years. I believe we're entitled. Colonel Duncan's agreed to it."

"Is there a way on earth we can stop you, Jake?" Rebecca asked.

"Not me, ma'am," Jake said, gazing around the table. "I guess you could stop them," he added, nodding to each of his brothers in turn. "They owe you for looking after 'em."

"We do," Jericho readily admitted. "Jake's right, though, Miz Selwyn. We've had about all the schooling a body can properly abide for a time. We won't all of us ever be needed on this farm. Time'll come when we need to make our own way. Best we learn how to work cows. Most say it's a trade a man can make his fortune at."

"Sooner or later you boys will be leaving," Selwyn said soberly. "I guess even our little Joel's time will arrive by and by. It makes sense you ought to ride out with Jake. All I ask is that you take care of yourselves. And if you don't drown in some river or get trampled by a rogue steer, come back and pass the winter with us. You'll always have a home here."

"We appreciate that, sir," Jericho said, speaking for them all.

"You figure you can spare me, too, Frank?" Si asked. "I wouldn't want to leave you short-handed, but—"

"Si, you're never any real help!" Rebecca exclaimed. "You only work one day in three. Go on. Keep Jericho from roping all the horses in Texas."

"You know we all appreciate everything," Jake told the Selwyns.

"Didn't do it for appreciation," Rebecca grumbled. "I love the all of you like my own. Just watch out and come back to see me."

"We will," Josh vowed.

Jordy rose from his chair and stepped over to give her a reassuring hug. Josh did likewise, and even Jericho, who was growing right out of his trousers, managed a farewell kiss.

Later, after the table had been cleared, the Wetherby brothers began gathering up their few spare shirts and rolling them in blankets. Rebecca Selwyn inspected each, and she brought Josh an extra pair of wool stockings.

"You know you take on chills when your feet are wet," she told the youngster. "Whenever you cross a river, you switch off your wet ones for the dry spare pair."

"Yes'm," Josh promised.

She went on offering advice and admonishing Jordy and Josh to mind their elders. Jake stepped outside and helped Si hitch two mules to a wagon.

"Want me to tie my roan along behind?" Si asked.

"That poor ol' horse won't make it north," Jake declared, frowning at the nag. "Colonel Duncan'll have horses for you. Best throw your saddle in back, though."

"Sure," Si agreed as he heaved the saddle onto one shoulder and carried it to the wagon. "Wouldn't do to rub my backside raw on new leather."

"No," Jake said, shaking his head. "Besides, horses are easier come by. I paid Marty fifty dollars to make saddles for the brothers. And that's with him being married to Jane Mary!"

"A brother-in-law's entitled to a profit, too, don't you think?" Si asked.

"I guess," Jake admitted as he strapped the mules in place. "But I confess I would have welcomed some charity just the same."

In truth, though, he looked forward to handing out those saddles. And no less an authority than John Duncan himself had congratulated Jake on the bargain price he'd managed for such fine leather work.

Si climbed atop the wagon and took the mules in hand. Jericho led his two smaller brothers out, and the three of them loaded their gear in the bed and crawled in behind. Jake then mounted Maizy and led the way west.

"It'll be a real adventure, won't it, Jake?" Jericho called from the back of the wagon.

"You know it will be," Jake answered, slapping his hat against his leg and howling like a coyote.

"Ayyyy!" his brothers echoed.

The sound echoed up Spring Creek and carried halfway to Colonel John Duncan's stagecoach station.

2

Duncan's Station stood astride the Preston Road, just the other side of a winding branch of White Rock Creek. There was a spring just beyond that offered a dependable water supply, both for the creek and the station, and it was a favorite layover for southbound travelers even before John Duncan had erected his station.

The place itself wasn't anything to boast about. There was a good stable and a wood corral, but the two-story plank station served the Duncans as home, inn, office, and warehouse. Still, it was grand for Collin County, and Jake always felt a tinge of envy when gazing upon the place.

"Yeah, the colonel's done all right by himself," his sister Jane Mary had remarked a few weeks before. "By you, too, Jake, judging by what folks say."

"He's been a good man to follow," Jake had agreed. "But I guess I've earned my pay."

He had, too. Nobody had ever accused Duncan of generosity. The colonel was honest, though, and he stuck by his friends. Jake numbered himself one.

When he rode up to the station, Jake was surprised to see the colonel out front, gabbing with a short, wiry young man beside the corral.

"Howdy, Colonel!" Jake called as he turned Maizy to the left. After stroking her neck, he took a deep breath and dismounted.

"This is the boy I mentioned, Wash," Duncan said, leading his companion toward Jake. "Jacob Henry Wetherby. A

11

bit hard-headed, and known to torment his elders on occasion, but a fair hand with horses.''

"And getting to halfway know cows," Jake boasted as he shook Duncan's hand.

"This is my nephew, George Washington Duncan," the colonel said, nodding to the thin man at his elbow.

"Glad to meet you, sir," Jake said, offering the younger Duncan a hand. Wash Duncan ignored it. Instead he gazed at the wagon lumbering toward the corral.

"Brought your brothers for a visit, I see," the colonel observed.

"Actually, Colonel," Jake said, taking another deep breath, "I, uh, thought maybe they'd be some help on the trail. You said I ought to look out for some boys to join the outfit. They'll work cheap, and—"

"Lord, Jake, I didn't mean children," the colonel grumbled. "Si there and Jericho maybe. Those other two—"

"We haven't stocked any diapers," Wash said, laughing. "Boy, we've got a lot of miles to cover. Hard miles."

"I know how many miles," Jake answered, gazing at the younger Duncan with icy eyes. "So do they. Came out from Tennessee and walked most all the way. As to hard, they might could teach you a thing about that."

"Jake!" the colonel barked.

Jake hung his head and retreated a step. He knew he was speaking out of turn, but it tore at him, hearing that dandified newcomer talking about diapers. By the look of him, Wash Duncan wasn't accustomed to any rough living himself. His hands were smooth—not a blister or callus in sight. His nails were trimmed and filed like an Austin lawyer's, and he smelled of lilacs.

"We need men," the colonel said, softening his tone. "Hard to come by these days, it appears. I turned two youngsters back this morning, and at least they had some acquaintance with a razor."

"You told me yourself, Colonel," Jake countered, "isn't how many chin hairs a man can boast that counts. It's what he can do with a rope. How long he can ride. I wasn't much older'n Jordy when I rode with you to the Brazos country hunting cows. Josh's small, I'll admit, but he'll have brothers to keep an eye on him, and he's good company. Si and Jer, well, they're a trial most times, but I'd want 'em with me in a tight place.''

"Kids," Wash muttered. "Uncle John, you can't—"

"I can't what?" Colonel Duncan asked. "Maybe I'm mistaken. You have a crew gathered up, son? A dozen or so rock-bottomed cow hunters hidden out past the creek maybe.''

"There have to be men hereabouts," Wash argued.

"Most have farms and families to tend," Jake explained. "Others plan to trail their own cows north. There are some, but the colonel isn't known for his free ways with silver."

"Deem yourself underpaid, do you, Jake?" Colonel Duncan asked.

"Not me," Jake said, painting a grin on his face. "My sister says you're a fool to keep me around. All I'm good for's chasing horses and roping cows. Me, I'd judge those selling points.''

"How many horses have those youngsters chased?" the colonel asked, pointing to little Josh in particular.

"Oh, they've chased quite a few," Jake declared. "Not caught any, but they've chased plenty.''

Colonel Duncan grinned in spite of himself. Wash frowned.

"We need a reliable crew, Uncle John," Wash insisted.

"Sure do," Jake quickly agreed. "Tell you what, Colonel. You judge for yourself. If my brothers don't prove themselves to you this first week, I'll take 'em back to Miz Selwyn myself. If they measure up, you pay 'em what you consider fair. Put three horses into the deal, and they'll be happy whatever it is.''

"I don't know, Jake," the colonel said, gazing at the boys. "Those little ones—"

"Are Wetherbys," Jake insisted. "They'll grow. Plenty of backbone to add to. Look, Colonel, I haven't asked much of you, and I figure you know I'm one to back up my words.

We haven't had much time, the four of us. Once Pa died, they split us up. A boy needs a nudge up the trail from somebody. Pa being gone, it's my job to do it. Give us this chance, and you won't regret it. Got my word on that.''

"They can stay for now, then," the colonel replied. "Through roundup. Afterward we'll talk some more.''

"Yes, sir," Jake said, nodding his thanks.

"Don't make me sorry," Colonel Duncan added.

"Haven't yet, have I?" Jake asked.

"Nobody does it twice, Jake," the colonel warned. "I can head north shorthanded if I have to.''

"I understand, sir," Jake said, gazing first at John Duncan's wrinkled brow and then taking note of the red tinge spreading across Wash's neck. Jake deemed it a poor bargain, making an enemy on such short acquaintance.

"Get them to stash their gear in the stable," Colonel Duncan finally announced. "Then get Frank Selwyn's wagon back to him.''

"I'll send Si to do it," Jake replied. "Anything else, Colonel?''

"Rest up," John Duncan urged. "You'll have hard work waiting for you tomorrow.''

"Yes, sir," Jake noted.

Once his brothers collected their gear, Jake tied a spare horse behind the wagon.

"I'll look after your outfit, Si," Jericho pledged.

"Don't go rolling my blankets in cow dung," Si warned. "I can get downright dangerous when riled.''

"Get along, Si," Jake urged. "Best you're back before dark.''

"Watch my gear, won't you, Jake?''

"Sure," Jake agreed. "Don't worry too much. There'll be no time for pranks tonight.''

Young Garrett then nudged the mules into motion, and the wagon rolled eastward. Jake waved his brothers toward the stable. They trudged inside, climbed a splintery ladder, and began stashing their gear in the loft.

"Not much of a home, huh?" Jake asked as they spread

out their blankets. He expected a grin. A trace of laughter even. Instead his brothers scowled.

"All right," Jake said, growing solemn. "What's wrong?"

"Diapers!" Josh grumbled. "Been a long time since anybody needed to wipe my rear!"

"You heard, huh?" Jake asked, laughing.

"I don't think it's a bad notion myself," Jordy said, pulling his smaller brother over. "By the look of that Wash fellow, he's apt to need some attention himself."

"You can't take it to heart, Peanut," Jake added. "You *are* on the small side. I was myself when I first signed on with the colonel. You'll take some ribbing until the other fellows figure you can hold your own."

"And till then?" Josh asked.

"Snarl at 'em," Jake advised. "Prank 'em when it's needed. Mostly, though, you do what you're supposed to and don't let the hurt show."

"Not much different than at school," Jordy noted. "After Pa died, the others took to pounding on us regular. Not always with hands, but sometimes words can hurt as bad."

"Sometimes," Josh agreed.

"Most times," Jake added. "I wanted to be there to help, you know. I am this time. Won't anybody bother you much here."

"They will or they won't," Jericho argued. "You can't help it, Jake. It's how people are. Being together's going to help some, but don't figure to do all the scrapping for us."

"We can hold our own," Jordy declared, staring coldly out the loft window. "We learned that pretty good the past couple of years."

"I want this summer to be better," Jake told them. "Easier."

"Jake, when did you ever know things to get easier?" Jericho asked. "Now, what should we do with ourselves while we wait for night to fall?"

"Don't know for certain," Jake confessed. "But I guess there's work to put our hands to. Always is around here."

Jake then led his brothers down to the stable floor. Two black men were busily raking muck from the stalls, and Jordy started to grab an idle pitchfork.

"Leave that to them," Jake barked.

"That's right," the taller of the two, a bony-armed giant named Nathaniel, said, turning toward the brothers. "This is our place. Mine and Jefferson's. We give you leave to sleep up there in the loft with Jake, but don't go messin' with our horses."

"Just meant to help," Jordy explained.

Nathaniel flashed a frown, and Jake hurried his brothers outside.

"He means it," Jake told them. "Those two have been together a long time. Now they're grown, the colonel says one of 'em can tend the horses. They're worried he'll sell one of 'em off."

"They're slaves, then," Jericho said, frowning. "I never much held—"

"Held?" Jake cried. "Hold your tongue and your thinking both. This isn't our place, Jer. What the colonel does is his business."

"I don't know I agree," Jericho argued.

"Jer's gone and turned abolitionist on us," Jordy explained.

"Well, I don't know I hold with owning people myself," Jake muttered. "But around here, I keep my mouth shut. I plan to trail cattle this summer, and that means working for John Duncan. You take a man's money, you respect his views."

"I guess," Jericho said, sighing.

"Now, let's see if we can help with the ponies," Jake said, motioning his brothers toward the corral. Even as they headed that way, three horsemen were driving two dozen horses through the gate. Jake waved, and they responded in like fashion.

"These your brothers?" a raven-haired young man in his early twenties asked as he climbed off a big sorrel.

"Eddie Stuart, meet the Wetherbys," Jake said, introducing each brother in turn. Afterward, Eddie offered his hand. When the other riders had tended to their mounts, they trotted over.

"We're Eddie's brothers," a grinning young man of nineteen explained. "I'm Gene."

"I'm Sylvester," a younger Stuart explained as he shook hands with the newcomers. "Poor name for a wrangler, wouldn't you say? Folks call me Tip."

"Howdy, Tip," Jericho said, stepping over so the two stood eyeball to eyeball. There wasn't a hair's difference in their heights.

"I'm seventeen," Jericho declared.

"You got a year on me," Tip said, sighing. "Glad you other Wetherbys come along. I was afraid I'd be the youngest. That's a purified nightmare, I can tell you."

"We can't be sure we're going yet," Jordy confessed.

"Colonel Duncan wasn't too sold on the notion," Jake explained.

"Oh, you'll go, all right," Tip assured them. "Long as you can still walk. Unless you get smarter the next week or so. No grown man's going to sign up with John Duncan when others offer better wages."

"Ah, he pays well enough," Jake argued.

"Less'n about everybody," Gene complained. "But he'll give you the use of a horse, and he feeds you. Doesn't hold your folks against you, either."

"We've got no folks," Jericho mumbled.

"I know," Gene said, wiping his brow with a kerchief. "You lost 'em early. Me, too. Only your pa didn't get himself hung for borrowin' horses."

"Yeah, you can say one thing 'bout the colonel," Tip declared. "He ain't afraid to give a fellow a leg up. A chance. You start with a clean slate with him. Just watch you don't disappoint him. He's no man you'd want for an enemy."

"No, that's a rare truth," Jake agreed.

"You need any help with those horses?" Jordy asked, hopping over to the corral and climbing the rails.

"You can brush down my sorrel there if you like," Eddie called from the far side of the corral.

"There's oats in the stable for the saddle horses and hay for the others," Gene explained. "You could bring some along to the feed troughs."

"Come on, Josh," Jericho said, leading his smaller brother toward the stable.

"Brush's in the tack room," Jake told Jordy.

Instantly Jordy raced along to fetch it.

"They're downright enthusiastic," Eddie observed as Jake helped him shoulder a saddle.

"Been too long on a farm, chopping wood and slopping hogs," Jake explained. "For them, this is pure adventure."

"The newness'll wear off," Eddie said, laughing.

"We were all tenderfeet once," Jake noted. "Even you, Eddie."

"Sure," Eddie agreed. "Trouble is, seein' half-pints like that, I feel altogether aged."

"Me, too, sometimes," Jake confessed. "Other times they shake me out of my boots and make me feel little all over."

"Listen to us," Eddie said, laughing. "Couple of old-timers, aren't we? Gray-headed and bent over."

"Not just yet," Jake declared as he grabbed a saddle blanket.

" 'Fore we get Colonel Duncan's cattle to market, we may feel that way, though," Eddie said, groaning. "Especially with that nephew o' his along."

"He'll watch himself," Jake argued. "I suspect he's got more to lose than anybody, what with the colonel having nobody but Miranda to will all his money to."

"Give me a Miranda Duncan any day," Eddie declared. "Wish it was her that was goin' along."

"Not me," Jake said, laughing. "She's harder'n the colonel to work for."

"Ten times as pretty, too," Eddie added. "Wouldn't any of us have time to work cows. Be too busy courtin'."

"Yeah, there's that, too," Jake said, grinning.

3

A bit later, after the horses had been tended and Oi Garrott had returned from his uncle's place, Jake led his brothers past the stable to a small rise where the Stuart brothers had made their camp.

"Time you met the rest of the crew," Jake explained.

He then introduced his brothers around. The others greeted Si and Jericho warmly enough, but Jake noticed they held back a hair from Jordy and Josh.

"It's a long ways through the Indian Nations to St. Louis," Ron Callahan, a gangly fellow from Tarrant County, told Jake. "You haven't trailed cows up there yourself. It's bound to be a trial."

"Will be," a shaggy-haired teen named Tyler Wells added. "We were all of us young once, though, Ron."

"Once?" Callahan cried. "How old are you now, Ty? Seventeen?"

"Nineteen," Ty growled. "Tall as you, too."

"My family tends toward runts, though," Callahan replied. "What's your excuse?"

If Jake hadn't known better, he would have judged the pair to be mortal enemies. In truth, they had been neighbors on the Trinity, and some would have guessed them brothers at first glance.

"Everybody hereabouts squabble like that?" Jordy asked.

"Sure," Tip Stuart explained. "It's workin' with cows does it to a man. Pure addles his brain, if you ask me."

"You'd be the one to know, little brother," Eddie remarked.

19

While the Stuarts wrestled around, Jake walked over to a small campfire and settled in beside Ron Callahan.

"Where are the others?" Jake whispered.

"Cook's due in tomorrow," Callahan explained. "The colonel's nephew brought a fellow along, but neither of them cared for our company. Miz Duncan's put 'em up at the station."

"Lofland's not here yet, either," Jake noted.

"Oh, he'll join us in Sherman. He didn't sign on to brand cows, Jake. His work begins once we start north."

"We're short on help," Jake muttered.

"I'd say so," Callahan agreed. "We might pick up a man or two in Grayson County, but you're lookin' at the roundup outfit."

"Wash Duncan can help with that, though."

"Can," Callahan grumbled. "Won't. I seen that sort plenty o' times. Long on wind and short on backbone. Your brothers used to workin' cattle?"

"No," Jake confessed. "They'll learn, though."

"They'll have to," Callahan added. "Best get 'em along to bed early. Dawn'll catch 'em dreamin'."

"No, they're used to rising with the roosters," Jake declared. But it was closing in on dusk, and Jake deemed it wise to return to the stable.

They passed a rather restless night there. Jake woke twice—once when Josh rolled over against him and a second time when a nightmare threw the boy into a fit. It took Jake and Jordy together to halt Josh's flaying arms and settle him down.

"I dreamed I got trampled by a bull," Josh explained when he got control of his breathing.

"No bulls up here in the loft," Jake assured his brother.

Josh nodded. In a few minutes he was fast asleep.

"Happen often?" Jake asked Jordy.

"Not in a while," Jordy explained. "A lot when we first went to the Selwyns."

Jake frowned. Staring at Josh, curled up in his nest of straw, Jake couldn't help wondering if he wasn't pushing the youngster onto too rugged a trail. He promised himself to watch his brothers closely during the roundup. If they showed signs of breaking down, Jake would return them to the Selwyns.

Morning came early. Jake blinked his eyes awake as yellow light streamed in through the loft window. Down below, Nathaniel and Jefferson were already at work.

"Aim to sleep forever?" Jordy called as he rolled his blankets up and set them near the window.

"Would if I could," Jake admitted. "But we've got work waiting."

"Breakfast, too, by the smell of things," Jericho observed.

"Only if we're presentable," Jake explained as he threw off his blanket and grabbed his trousers. He wasted no time getting dressed and stowing his bedding. Then he led his brothers down the ladder, out of the stable, and on past the station house to where Miranda Duncan had set up a washbasin.

"Miz Duncan fussy, is she?" Jordy asked as he dipped a cloth into the water and began scrubbing the sweat and grime from his face.

"She does require a bath now and then," Jake admitted. "With so many cows and horses around, I don't guess you can blame her for wanting the human beings to smell a little better."

"Lot of wasted effort, if you ask me," Josh grumbled.

"That's 'cause you don't remember her too well, Peanut," Jake declared. "I know at your age, you might not care about a woman's smile, but you haven't tasted her cooking. Pretty soon you'll be chewing cold biscuits and tinned beans. A Miranda Duncan meal's worth a little inconvenience."

"I'll admit I could eat something," Josh said, grinning.

After inspecting faces and hands, Jake led his little company to the station. The Stuarts were already sitting at one table, gobbling platters of ham, sausage, and eggs. Jake made his way past them to where Ty Wells and Ron Callahan were sipping coffee.

"Mornin', Wetherbys," Ty said.

"Morning," Jake replied.

Josh and Jordy occupied the remaining two chairs. Si and Jericho sat at a third table.

"Best eat up," Ty urged. "We'll be out at roundup the next week or so."

"Dry beef and cold biscuits," Callahan grumbled. "Josh, fatten yourself up good. The way you are now, first good wind'll blow you straight to Mexico."

"Naw," Josh said, shaking his head. "Kansas maybe, but never Mexico. Wind's out of the south in springtime."

Jake couldn't resist laughing.

"This boy'll do," Callahan observed.

Miranda Duncan then appeared with a platter of steaming biscuits, and Jake grew silent.

"I see you brought your whole family, Jacob Henry," she said as she set down the platter.

"Just about," Jake replied.

She'd always been pretty. At first glance he had suspected her frail, but he'd learned better those past months. She wasn't much more than three inches past five feet tall, and it would be generous to guess eighty pounds were painted onto her thin frame. Hard work had put iron in her wrists, and she could ride most men, Jake Wetherby included, right into the dust.

"I believe you've grown, Jordy," she observed, squeezing his shoulders. "And this here can't be Josh. Why, he's grown half a foot since February!"

"More like an inch," Josh said, biting the corner off a biscuit.

"I've got some flapjacks for you boys," Miranda declared. "Sausage, ham, and plenty of eggs."

"You bring 'em, ma'am," Jordy said. "We'll see they're eaten."

"I imagine you will," she said, laughing.

Miranda then turned and headed back to the stove. She returned shortly with more food, and soon Jake and his brothers were occupied stuffing themselves.

"She's outdone herself," Ty noted as he stabbed a sausage link with his fork and prepared to bite off one end.

"She puts even Miz Selwyn to shame," Josh declared.

"Hard to do, too, when she's cooking for a dozen hands," Jordy observed.

"She's used to that," Jake explained. "Feeds the stage passengers when they lay over."

Even so, Jake reasoned Miranda put a little extra effort into that breakfast.

"They've got hard times ahead," she told Jake when he helped her carry out a second platter. "It's best they start with full stomachs."

"Like as not, we'll have to sew up split-out trousers, though," Jake observed.

"I've got some things set aside for them," she explained, gazing around the room with her bright blue eyes. "Clothes left behind by guests. Unclaimed freight."

Jake nodded. It was an old game of Miranda's. She was always happening across things needed by Jake and his brothers. Just before their father died, she sent out a stack of school slates. Later Jake discovered she'd sent all the way to St. Louis for them.

"Thanks," he said, squeezing her hand.

"You know how it is," she whispered. "These things just take up space. Besides, I don't have any brothers of my own."

"Just as well," Jake told her. "You wouldn't have half so kind a heart after they pranked and tormented you."

"I don't know I wouldn't accept that as the price, Jake."

"Sure," he said, laughing as Jordy tried to swallow a biscuit in one gulp. "It's no good, being alone."

Jake knew there was scant chance of that happening those next few days. There was so much to do. So many things to teach the boys. Even as Miranda was handing out shirts and such, Jake was lugging saddles out of the tack room.

"Can't be a proper cowboy without a horse," Eddie told the newcomers. "Best pick out a pony and bring him on out of the corral."

"Sure," Jordy said, climbing the rails and jumping down

into the corral. The others followed, but Jordy insisted on picking out the horses for each of them.

"That boy knows ponies," Tip Stuart said, scratching his chin. "He's got the makings of a wrangler in him."

"Has a way with critters," Jake explained. "Always has. He rides better than most, too. Hasn't had a lot of practice, I'll admit, but he'll pass muster."

"Better'n some," Ty said, laughing as Jericho tried to coax a spotted gelding out of the corral.

"Take a firm hand, Jer!" Jordy barked. "No, like this," he added, giving the gelding a light tap on the rump.

Afterward, as Tip handed out saddle blankets, Jake presented the saddles.

"This's got my name tooled in the side!" Josh exclaimed.

"Present from me and Marty," Jake explained.

"Now I know why he was measuring us back in April," Jericho said, laughing. "Thought for certain Jane Mary intended sewing us some more of those canvas britches."

"Not after those first ones," Jordy said, laughing. "You could've put the whole family in the seat of my pants."

"Made for proper shelters, though," Josh argued.

Jake couldn't help grinning. He quickly quieted them, though. With Ty and Tip helping, he instructed his brothers in the fine art of saddling their horses. Jordy listened good-naturedly and then went right to it. Josh struggled to get his saddle atop a painted mare. Jericho managed to get his saddle in place, but Jake had to tighten the cinch. As for Si, he had his horse saddled just fine, but when he climbed up, saddle and rider both rolled halfway off the side.

"Helps to tighten her a hair," Tip said, laughing.

Once they were all mounted, Jake waited for Eddie to take charge. He didn't. Instead Wash Duncan rode up with a sandy-haired young man of twenty named Martin Albert.

"You've been fed and mounted," Wash growled. "Now it's time you earn your keep."

"That's why we're here," Eddie replied.

"Sure, boss," Tyler Wells added. "Let's get started."

John Duncan had brought a few hundred head in from his

land holdings farther west, but northern Texas was full of stray cattle, and the colonel expected to build his herd considerably.

"I expect us to gather three thousand head easy!" Wash boasted.

"Too many to handle on the trail," Eddie grumbled later when he and Jake coaxed a trio of cows out of a ravine. "You won't want to take calves up there, either."

"Be a considerable number to brand even so," Jake muttered.

"Enough so we'll feel ourselves stomped on and dusted over."

As if that wasn't enough, Colonel Duncan set out north and east, buying up any longhorns he could at three or four dollars a head.

"Not much of a price by Missouri standards, but it's a second cash crop for some of those farmers," Eddie Stuart noted. "My brothers and I brought in sixty we chased down west of Sherman. Colonel gave me a hundred dollars, and I consider it easy money for a day's ridin'."

Jake thought so, too, but once they were out of sight of the station and out in the wilds, he began to have his doubts. The land was wild, hostile. There were a thousand perils at hand. Jake recalled hunting mustangs in that country.

"Ran across Indians not far from here," Jake told Eddie.

"I'll keep that in mind," Eddie vowed.

But it was Wash who managed the roundup. Where before Colonel Duncan sent the men out in small bands to collect cattle, Wash used different tactics. He led the way to a small creek with good grass on both banks. Jake had barely caught his breath when he spied a chuck wagon approaching from the east.

"The cook," Eddie announced.

Indeed, that was just who it was, too. Doc Trimble, a one-legged veteran of the Mexican War, called out to them from the wagon, and Wash led them closer.

"Howdy, boys!" Doc shouted.

"You're late," Wash grumbled.

"I wasn't due to cook anything 'fore noon," Trimble replied. "Been speakin' with the colonel."

"I expected you to—"

"Look, young fellow, I never made any bargain with you," Trimble barked. "I ain't much on ridin' horses nor chasin' cows, but I'll keep you fed. Sew you up when you get split open, dose your ailments, and sing the babies to sleep. I take my orders from the colonel, though."

Jake noticed approving grins appearing on other faces. The Stuarts, Callahan . . .

"Best you understand who's in charge here," Wash insisted.

"I guess I know," Trimble replied. "Now, you want to stand here and argue, or do you plan to get this roundup started?"

4

Wash Duncan's notion was to move the camp through the flats, gathering in longhorns each morning and branding them the same afternoon. It was a good enough notion, Jake supposed, except it meant containing the herd at the same time they were rounding up strays and working the stock. Cow hunting was long, tedious work anytime, and with the sun blazing down, it gradually broke a man down. Coupling such labor with the exhausting task of roping and branding seemed insane.

"It's worked elsewhere," Wash argued as he paired the men up. "Once you finish handling the breeding stock, you release them back onto the range. Only the trail herd needs to be kept together."

"Trouble is, the cows won't understand," Ty objected. "They got a habit of sticking together."

"Another thing," Eddie said, sighing. "We've got too many youngsters to spread ourselves so thin. Most have to learn it all. You go and swap tasks too often, they won't do any of it very well."

"I warned Uncle John about taking on all those children," Wash grumbled. "Well, you boys best learn fast. This is a job that'll get done with or without you. Anybody doesn't hold up his end gets paid off. Understand?"

"Won't get the job done, though," Eddie complained.

Jake didn't bother arguing. He'd known plenty of men like Wash Duncan. Once they set their cap, there was no convincing them otherwise. Instead he devoted himself to working with his brothers, braiding lariats for them to use, and passing on a trick or two Jake had picked up out west.

"Thing to keep in mind is these fool critters can kill you," Jake admonished when he was through. "A horn can rip right through a horse's lungs. Can tear your leg off, too. You keep clear of the horns no matter what."

"Other thing to remember is to leave the bulls to us," Gene declared. "A good cow pony can control an animal better than the finest roper you ever saw. You boys'll do well to keep atop these ponies you're ridin'."

Just the same, the youngsters were a lot of help. The hours of pounding across ravines and ridges didn't seem to drown their spirits. Jake finished each morning worn down to a nub and caked in dust. He rode into camp like a gray-tinged ghost, and when he bathed in the creek each evening, he discovered grit in places he hadn't imagined possible.

Having his brothers along, Jake refused to admit his own fatigue. The days squeezed Josh into a limp washrag, and they broke down Jordy and Jer, too. Only Si Garrett seemed immune to the hardships.

"It's because he's the laziest person I ever saw," Tip Stuart noted.

Jake only shook his head. Si was a prankster, and no one had ever accused him of overwork. Still, he was learning how to let his horse drive the cattle, and he was becoming adept at coaxing animals out of ravines.

Jordy, too, was demonstrating a talent for cow hunting. For a boy not much more than five feet tall, he had a voice that boomed halfway across the county. His rope work was accurate, and he was quicker to drop a loop over a cow's head than anybody in the outfit.

"That boy's comin' along," Eddie declared when Jordy pulled in a reluctant bull. "He'll make a good cowboy once his bottom gets used to a saddle."

Jake laughed later when he noticed Jordy sitting naked in the creek, letting the cold river salve his tormented flesh.

It wasn't exciting, those long hours rounding up cattle. Sometimes they brought in small groups of two or three. At

most ten. Other mornings they scoured a half-dozen ridges
and ravines without locating two dozen longhorns. Worst of
all, many good cows turned out to be branded strays off
nearby ranches. Colonel Duncan was obligated to turn over
such animals, and the only reward the cow hunters got was
an occasional peach pie or a nod from some rancher's wife.

While the work wearied a man, sapping his strength and
numbing his senses, it could never be taken lightly. A longhorn didn't come by its name by chance. Some of the mavericks sported horns four or more feet long from tip to tip.
A sudden move in an unexpected direction could spell disas-
ter for a cowboy. He might easily have a leg split open from
knee to crotch. Tip Stuart lost a good horse the second day
when a longhorn cow attacked, swinging its wicked horns
wildly and gutting the poor mare with rare ferocity.

Tip himself was trapped beneath his horse, and if Jake and
Eddie hadn't raced over and shot the vicious cow, the boy
might have suffered as grim a fate.

"Won't be much longer men try to drive these ornery
critters north," Eddie declared afterward. "People are
comin' north and west, settlin' the land. Once they're there,
range cattle are sure to disappear. No grass left for 'em. No
open country."

Jake hoped the day would wait. Currently a man could
amass a small fortune running a herd on the open range. He
didn't need thousands of acres or a tall house. All it took was
a small band of friends to run down the animals, and a good
outfit to drive them north to markets in Missouri and Kansas.

Just when the drudgery began to wear him down, Jake
spied a rogue bull stuck in an old buffalo wallow. The longhorn bellowed angrily as it tried to free its feet.

"Bet you a dollar you can't run down there and pull that
old bull's tail," Si told Jericho.

"You crazy?" Jericho cried. "Look at his horns! He'd
start out by poking you a new belly button and then maybe
tear off an elbow or knee."

"Naw, he's stuck," Si insisted. "You afraid? Fine. Offer
me the same bet."

"You're crazy!" Jericho argued.

"Bet?" Si asked, grinning.

"Don't you have some crazy superstition about messing with bulls?"

"Naw, I never heard a one. I'll run down there and have a tug at its tail. Then I get the dollar, right?"

"And more besides," Jericho said, laughing. "Go ahead and try, though. I got a dollar, and I figure it would be worth it to see you run around, squealing like a stuck piglet."

Si laughed at the taunt and climbed down from his horse. With rare caution, he sidled up to the bull, humming an old church hymn. The music seemed to calm the bull for a moment, and it quit struggling. Instead it took a couple of forceful steps. Si failed to notice the bull escaping the wallow. No longer working against the suction of the mire, the longhorn was regaining its freedom.

"Si?" Jericho called out.

"Si, don't!" Jake warned.

Si was nothing if not audacious. He not only lifted the bull's tail, but he gave the poor creature a quick poke with a willow limb.

The bull thundered its outrage and turned with a suddenness that caught Si off balance. He lost hold of the tail and went sprawling in the muck. The bull, meanwhile, had completed its turn and was pawing at the ground, angrily snorting as it eyed Si's helpless form.

"Help!" Si screamed as the bull started its charge.

Si could see death coming, and he wasted no time regaining his feet and commencing a frantic run. At first the wallow slowed him some, but it kept the bull behind, too. Once clear of the bog, Si headed up a small slope toward a stand of cottonwoods. The bull closed. A hundred feet short of the trees the bull lowered his head and butted Si right off the ground. If he had been ten pounds heavier, Si would have fallen right onto the bull's deadly horns. Instead he flew toward the trees and managed to scramble along to safety.

By then the bull stood on the slope, confused.

"I've got to get Si," Jericho called, turning his horse toward the trees.

Jake winced. The bull blocked Jericho's path, and the animal immediately started toward the approaching rider. Now there was only one thing Jake could do. Sighing, he drew his Sharps rifle from its saddle scabbard and advanced a cartridge into its chamber. He hated killing that old bull. Some things are meant to remain wild, in the open, unfettered and untroubled by the world beyond their eyes. There was no way an inexperienced horseman like Jer could avoid that bull, though. Better for the bull to die than for Jake to lose a brother.

Jake took aim and grimly fired. The bullet struck the bull's flank and tore into a lung. Staggered but far from dead, the bull continued. Jake's second shot halted the longhorn's charge forever.

"Fine shot, that one!" Eddie Stuart shouted as he emerged from a nearby ravine.

"Equal of any I ever saw," Gene agreed as he joined his brother. "Heard you held your own fightin' Kiowas with the colonel out on the Brazos."

"Didn't do much," Jake said, sighing. "Shooting longhorns with a Sharps, well, it wasn't me that was in danger."

"And Indians?" Eddie asked.

"Be just fine by me if I never shot at anybody the whole rest of my life," Jake declared, returning the rifle to its scabbard. "It's not at all what you expect. I near heaved my guts out when it was over. I'm still sick at my stomach over it."

"Nothing's ever what you expect," Eddie noted. "Come on. Let's butcher the bull. Have some fresh meat tonight for a change."

"I guess that would be welcome," Jake admitted.

After chastising Si and Jericho, Jake assisted the Stuarts with the butchering. They couldn't haul off even a quarter of the meat, and it troubled Jake some to be so wasteful.

"Birds'll have a good feed, Jake," Si declared as Jericho rubbed liniment into his bruised and battered friend's tailbone. "If I hadn't goaded that old bull into stepping out of the mud, he'd be there still. Buzzards would have ate every bit of him then.''

The bull's mad charge sobered the cow hunters, and thereafter Jake noticed his brothers gave the longhorns a considerably greater amount of respect. Losing a horse soured Wash Duncan some on Si, but the young man's sense of humor and exaggerated tales shared at evening campfire balanced the scales.

"I know, Colonel," Jake said when John Duncan arrived at the roundup camp later that week. "You'd like to send the whole bunch of us home, but few of us have one. We're shameless varmints, the whole bunch. But that's what it takes to get this sort of job done.''

"You may be right," Duncan admitted. "Before we start north, though, we have to have some discipline. We're too few to have any weak links on the trail.''

"We won't have any," Jake vowed. "At least not any named Wetherby.''

"And Si Garrett?''

"I'll watch him, too," Jake pledged.

If mornings were a trial, afternoons weren't any better. John Duncan was determined to start a thousand head north—the largest batch anybody had heard of—and keep the rest on open range north and west of the station. They began roundup with two hundred branded cattle, and they brought an average of another hundred in each morning.

"I'll be downright sick of this in no time," Eddie Stuart grumbled as he readied the branding irons. "I bet we've got fifteen hundred or so to mark. Lot of work. Boys, best fetch your knives, too. Half of 'em need cuttin'.''

"Cutting?" Josh asked.

"We take mostly steers north," Eddie explained. "We'll leave the older bulls and some bull calves, of course. Colonel Duncan will want breedin' stock.''

"You mean—" Josh began.

"Ah, Josh, we've done it with hogs plenty of times," Jordy declared. "Is it any different, Jake?

"Some," Jake confessed. "I'm no expert, of course.''

"Main difference is there's a lot of 'em,'' Tip said, shuddering. "You get to where you're sick of the blood and the wailin'. Your arms ache from holdin' down calves. And I got to be truthful. No man ever takes this sort of business all that lightly."

The others laughed nervously.

The first couple of days it seemed as if they would never get finished. Gene, Tip, and Ty handled most of the roping. Ron Callahan and Eddie dropped the animals and held them while Jake and the others took turns at the branding. It took some getting used to, pressing that hot iron down into the hide until it burned in a permanent brand. Eddie notched the ears himself, but Jericho and Si wound up with the other knife work.

"It's not so bad once you get used to it,'' Si boasted. "I almost believe I could do it in my sleep."

Jake laughed a bit when he noticed nobody spread his blankets anywhere near Si that night.

As for Josh, he mostly stood watch over the herd or helped Doc Trimble at the chuck wagon. Even so, he finished most days pale as a ghost, and even afternoon swims didn't revive the boy.

"Peanut, you all right?'' Jake asked.

"Got sick a couple of times,'' Josh finally confessed. "Took my turn at the branding. Pressing that hot iron into those poor cows' hides! And then I had to help Jordy cut some calves. Guess I don't have it in me to be a cowboy."

"It's hard sometimes,'' Jake said, allowing his little brother to edge closer. "I wouldn't think less of you if you wanted to wait for another summer. Miz Selwyn would welcome you back."

"I know,'' Josh said, clasping Jake's arm. "If it's up to me, though, I want to go. Tip says it'll get better. You can't cut much more off those calves. I'm not the greatest rider in Texas, but I'll work at it."

"I want you with us, Peanut,'' Jake declared. "But I worry I'm asking too much."

"No, I'm up to the trip,'' Josh said, managing a grin. "I

always wanted to see Missouri. Heard the mountains there are like Tennessee.''

''Guess we'll have to find out, Peanut.''

Later, after Josh took to his blankets, Jake had second thoughts. He set off down the creek alone, pondering the hazards that lurked on the trail north.

''You're mighty restless tonight, Jake,'' Eddie Stuart said as he stepped out of the darkness. ''We've got two more long days ahead of us and then weeks of hard riding. You need your rest.''

''Sure,'' Jake agreed.

''Worryin' over the brothers, huh?''

''You got two yourself,'' Jake said, frowning. ''I'm afraid I'm asking too much.''

''They say so?''

''Of course not,'' Jake said, shaking his head. ''Even if Jer had a horn through both lungs, he wouldn't admit he was hurt. And Jordy! He's mostly horse, that boy. Josh, though. He's been sickly since the day he was born. I—''

''Don't sell any of 'em short, Jake.''

''I'm not. Leastwise, I don't think so. My pa was a man that had a bad habit of expecting more than a boy could manage. Nobody ever measured up. I just hate to—''

''It's hard country, Texas,'' Eddie said, gazing up at the moon shining brightly overhead. ''She asks a powerful lot from all of us. My pa always hunted the easy road, and it didn't earn him much of an end. You wouldn't do your brothers any favor, holdin' 'em back, smoothin' out the way for 'em. Hard trails make hard men. There's pain, I grant you, but you learn to handle it. A soft man cracks up just when he needs to be strongest. He can't reach down deep and grab gumption because there were no tough times to grow it there.''

''I'd like to believe that.''

''Glance over at Wash Duncan and that Albert fellow that rides with him,'' Eddie suggested. ''How much work did we get from either of 'em?''

''Not much,'' Jake confessed.

"It's important you let those boys test themselves, Jake," Eddie insisted. "Even Josh. Only the strong get by in this life. Take that for the only truth I've ever discovered."

"The only trouble, Eddie, is that I've seen three brothers buried already," Jake explained. "If you're not strong enough, sometimes you just don't survive."

"True enough. But it's better to die tryin' than sit back in a hole, never testin' your mettle. At least you know what life tastes like."

"And death?"

"Finds us all in the end, my friend. Now let's get back to camp and get some rest."

"Sure," Jake agreed.

By the time the final week of May rolled around, close to two thousand cattle had been brought in and branded with the Bar JD brand favored by John Duncan. The colonel himself had inspected the stock and ordered a thousand head readied for the drive north. The others, including calves and their attending cows, had been chased west. Some two hundred cows remained. The other eight hundred were steers.

With the cattle assembled, Colonel Duncan turned to the crew. It was common practice to ring a herd with men, giving each a specific position. Colonel Duncan and Wash would lead the way. To Jake's dismay, Duncan allowed his nephew to assign the others their duties.

"Fool wouldn't know his head from his tail," Eddie Stuart grumbled when Wash gave Martin Albert the critical left point position. "You'll have a hard row to hoe, Jake."

Jake was to ride right point, and he understood only too well Eddie's complaint. The point riders were responsible for directing the herd. Albert had disappeared daily during the roundup, and Jake suspected he would trail along behind Wash Duncan and shirk his duties. That left Jake overburdened, and the swing riders, Gene Stuart and Ty Wells, would be hard-pressed to shape the herd and cut off strays. Eddie and Ron Callahan were assigned to ride the flanks, where their experience would pay off. Jericho, Jordy, and Si were given the unenviable task of riding drag—trailing the herd and coaxing stragglers along.

"Be chewing a lot of dust before summer's over," Doc Trimble told the youngsters.

As for the relief horses, Tip would have charge of the remuda. At his brother Eddie's suggestion, he kept the horses on the left, giving Eddie a chance to push Ty a hair farther up front and cover for Albert. Doc Trimble vowed to keep the supply wagon on that side as well.

"I wish I had a more experienced outfit," the colonel told Jake as they loaded provisions into the supply wagon.

"You said something about hiring a couple of riders up north," Jake said as he heaved a flour sack into the wagon.

"I spoke to a couple of hands, but they're just boys," Duncan explained. "I need a reliable man or two. Like the ones that went out west with us that first time."

"They're mostly dead," Jake observed. "Or broken down."

"Working stock has its drawbacks."

"Colonel, you haven't said anything about my brother Josh," Jake pointed out. "He's—"

"Pitiful small, Jacob Henry," Duncan broke in. "Wouldn't last the trip on horseback."

"Might surprise you, sir."

"Even Wash isn't fool enough to set that child to chasing strays or dodging stampedes. I know why you asked him along, Jake, and I consider it a fine notion."

"But?"

"A boy that small's put to better purpose than chewing dust and coughing out his life."

"You got something in mind?" Jake asked.

"Doc asked if he could sign Josh on as cook's helper," Colonel Duncan explained. "Be a lot of pot stirring and kettle scrubbing. Not much adventure."

"Nothing he hasn't done before," Jake noted. "Lots of new country to see. Doc wouldn't appear to be bad company, either."

"I'd appreciate you talking to the boy, then."

"Thanks, Colonel," Jake said, nodding respectfully. "I'll do it right now."

Josh was down at the creek, helping Jordy fill canteens, when Jake found him.

"Peanut, can you spare me a minute?" Jake called.

"Sure," Josh said, sighing.

They walked a few paces upstream before Jake stopped.

"I know," Josh mumbled. "You're sending me back to Miz Selwyn."

"That what you want?" Jake asked.

"You know better," Josh answered. His face grew hard and his eyes glared with rare fury. "I may not be tall, but I can rope cows better'n that Albert fellow. Or Wash Duncan. I've done my part, and I deserve a chance to go along."

"It would be hard on you, Peanut."

"You remember a time when it was easy?" Josh asked. "I know I've got things left to learn, but so do the others."

"I also know you never cared much for dust. I wouldn't care to hear you coughing like the night before last."

"There's other places to ride than drag, Jake."

"Now, that's an idea. Truth is, we've got a problem with old Doc. He thinks he's ill-treated, given all the work of cook and doc and quartermaster with no one to help."

"He asked me if I'd ever fried bacon," Josh remarked.

"He wants you to ride with him, be his assistant."

"Scrub pots, you mean."

"You don't think much of the notion, do you?"

"No, Jake. I figure it's fine. I'd be doing it back at the Selwyns', and this way I'll have more time to ponder pranks."

"We'll get you out riding from time to time, too," Jake vowed.

"I'll remember that," Josh said, grinning. "It's not such a bad bargain, Jake. Somebody in the family ought to learn to cook halfway decent. And we'll still have time to swim creeks and swap tales."

"Sure, we will," Jake agreed.

With that final matter resolved, Jake waved Josh back to Jordy and turned back to the wagon. He only got halfway there before Miranda Duncan grabbed his arm and led him aside.

"I guess you weren't going to bother saying good-bye," she scolded.

"I never was much good at it," he confessed. "Besides, we won't be gone forever."

"Just months," she complained.

"Eddie says we'll be so busy we'll lose track of the time."

"I won't," she argued. "You watch yourself, Jacob Henry Wetherby. If it was all that easy a thing to do, you'd see more men doing it. And there'd be no need for a Stan Lofland."

"Sure," he said, clasping her hands.

"Something else, too."

"Yeah?"

"You've been around Wash enough to judge him yourself. Don't let that fool get Papa hurt."

"I'll do what I can, but there's no arguing the colonel out of anything, Miranda. You'd know that better'n anybody."

"You know what I mean, Jake."

"Sure, and I'll stand by him. You didn't need to ask that."

"Maybe not. I'm downright certain you won't break a promise, not one you make to me, face-to-face."

"You're not really worried, are you?"

"Aren't you?" she asked. "Headed north with a bunch of boys! Lord help you, Jake. You're a graybeard by comparison."

"I'll be losing my teeth most any day now."

"Jake, stop that!" she howled as he laughed at the notion.

"Don't worry too much," Jake urged. "We may not be old, but there's not a one of us who doesn't understand his obligations. Leaving out your cousin, that is. We'll see this through. It's to our advantage, too, you see."

"Sure," she agreed.

"I'd best hurry up and help load that wagon now, Miranda," Jake said, holding her close a moment. "We'll be heading out pretty soon."

"Don't forget your promise," she urged as he turned away.

I never have, he silently replied.

They started north that same afternoon. It was difficult going at first. Stringing out a thousand head of cattle along the Preston Road required constant vigilance. Cows and steers tried to break away at every turn. The animals weren't accustomed to moving even small distances, and they fought to remain on familiar ground. Moreover, the land was scarred by gullies and shallow streams. Twice the lead steers turned westward, and once a batch of fifty or so broke past Martin Albert and escaped.

"Lord help us!" Gene Stuart cried as he rode up alongside Jake.

Together they managed to contain the main body, but there was no catching the strays.

"How many got away?" Colonel Duncan shouted as he and Wash rode up with Albert.

"Don't know for sure," Jake answered. "As few as fifty. Could be a hundred."

"We can't get ten miles north without trouble!" the colonel stormed. "Wash?"

"I told you we ought to put an older man up front," Wash said, glaring at Jake.

"They didn't break away on the right, Colonel," Gene argued. "Truth is, we swung over and cut off most of the critters. Got the lead steers in hand and turned the herd back up the road."

"Well, you weren't much help to me!" Albert growled.

"We weren't?" Gene countered. "Well, now where were you, anyhow?"

"A man's got the need to answer nature's call," Albert explained.

"Might be best to wait till you get past a creek crossing next time," Colonel Duncan said, frowning. "Anything keeping you from going after the strays?"

"Now?" Albert asked. "Alone? There could be Indians about!"

"Then you best get to my cattle before they do," Colonel Duncan thundered. "Wash, you go along with him, too. Once you see how much trouble's been caused, maybe you'll think about who you put at point."

"Uncle John, I—" Wash objected.

"It's not too late to pay a man off!" Colonel Duncan

barked. "Anyone. A man who takes his pay from me accepts responsibility for his mistakes. Atones for them, too."

"Sir?" Wash asked.

"We'll make camp on the far side of this creek," Colonel Duncan explained. "You round up those strays and rejoin us."

Wash started to complain, but a harsh scowl from his uncle froze him. Wash Duncan swallowed his words and turned his horse westward. Martin Albert trailed along behind.

"Those two'll never find the strays," Gene declared. "Colonel, you better send Eddie out after 'em."

"Already did," Duncan answered. "Jordy's seeing after the horses so Tip could go with his brother."

"Then why send Wash?" Jake asked.

"Because it's his mess, and he ought to clean it up," Duncan replied. "I'd leave it to him if it wasn't a hundred head."

"They won't either of them be any use to Eddie," Gene declared.

"Well, at least they'll be out of my sight for a few hours," Duncan explained. "And they can't lose us any other batch."

Jake thought he noticed a trace of a grin on the colonel's face just then, but if so, it didn't remain long. Instead the colonel began barking orders. Jake soon found himself busy directing the herd onto a section of rich prairie enclosed on three sides by a meandering creek. The cattle, freed of human prodding, were content to stand and graze.

"I'm leaving half the outfit on watch," Colonel Duncan told Jake as he rode around the rim of the herd. "Callahan will be in charge for now. You and those tenderfoot brothers of yours might take advantage of the fine weather we're having and wash some trail dust off in the creek."

"There'll be time for that later, Colonel," Jake pointed out. "We might should ride out and give Eddie a hand."

"You might do what I tell you," Duncan growled. "You said you wanted those boys coming along so you could share some time. Won't be many idle moments once we get ourselves moving."

"Yes, sir," Jake replied. "It's just, well, we didn't get you off to much of a beginning, and I—"

"Did your part, Jacob Henry. Leave Wash and Eddie to do theirs. Could be your brothers'll want a swim. Hasn't been an easy day for them, I suspect."

Jake nodded. Slowly he turned Maizy south and rode toward the settling dust that marked the tail end of the herd.

Jake felt a bit guilty, splashing away the late afternoon heat while others watched the herd. Still, it was a rare chance to chase his brothers through the shallows and escape the dust and smell of a thousand longhorns.

"I believe I'm almost human again," Jordy declared as he floated aimlessly on his back.

"I confess I can recognize you again," Jake said, shaking his head. "I never minded you acting halfway like a horse, but it was a little hard on the nose, smelling you."

The cooling waters of the creek revived little Josh, too. It tore some at Jake, seeing the boy shy of his clothes. He could count Josh's ribs when the boy hopped around, and Josh's eyes appeared red and withered with exhaustion.

"Peanut, you tell Doc to feed you double," Jake suggested.

"Oh, I'm not near as skinny as I used to be," Josh boasted, pushing out his belly. "When I first got to the Selwyns', I was so bony it was pitiful."

"I guess we didn't do so good a job looking after you," Jake said, sighing.

"You weren't much to boast about yourself, Jake," Jordy declared. "We all take after Ma's side of the family."

"Sure," Jake agreed, recalling his father's constant complaints. "Fitch runts! Long and lean."

"And none too long, either," Jericho muttered from the shallows. Jer never had been comfortable around water. Not after their five-year-old brother Jeremiah had drowned back in Tennessee.

"Some are tall all along," Jake noted as he swam toward the bank. "Others take their time at it. I'm getting my size, and you will, too."

Jericho started to grumble, but Jake grabbed an arm and pulled him along toward a deep pool.

"We've got a lot of rivers to cross going north," Jake whispered. "You might as well get used to water now. Build up your strokes. You'll be glad later."

"I'm not too handy in the water," Jericho argued.

"You weren't much good on a horse last week," Jake pointed out. "All you need's practice. Get at it!"

Jake and Jordy took turns racing Jericho down the creek. Josh, meanwhile, splashed his way to the bank and got himself dressed.

"Promised Doc to get along back and help with the cooking," the youngster explained.

Jake nodded approvingly.

"Kind of satisfying, seeing him grow," Jordy observed. "Ma always babied him, and Miz Selwyn picked up the habit. This'll be good for him."

"If it doesn't demand too much," Jake grumbled.

"He's thirteen, Jake," Jericho added. "He won't abide pampering from anybody. From you, in particular, I suspect."

"Is that what I'm doing?" Jake asked.

"No, but it's in you," Jordy declared. "Give him room. He won't disappoint you."

Jake nodded. He vowed to try, even though it would be hard.

They swam another quarter hour before spilling out of the creek. They then shook themselves dry, threw on their clothes, and relieved the others. Jake was glad he was on horseback when Eddie and Tip Stuart returned. They were soaked through with sweat and powdered with layers of dust. They did manage to collect forty-three strays, but the look in Eddie's eyes said it all. Others remained on the loose.

"Have a swim and a rest," Colonel Duncan told the Stuarts. "You did what you could. See Wash?"

"He and that fool Albert rode by, but neither offered any help," Eddie grumbled.

"I guess they headed after the others," Tip said, shying from the colonel's hard gaze.

"I trust so," Duncan growled. "I judge we're still shy forty head."

"You always lose some on the way north," Eddie insisted.

"Generally you get a herd to the Red River intact," Duncan replied. "At this rate, we won't have ten when we leave the Nations."

Jake was worried the colonel might be right. He wasn't a bit relieved when Wash and Martin Albert returned coaxing a pair of steers along.

"Found two, did you?" the colonel called as Wash climbed off his horse and headed for the cook wagon.

"I saw Stuart had the rest," Wash explained.

"All but forty," the colonel noted. "You and that young fool friend of yours only cost me a fifth of my profit."

"Uncle John, we—" Wash began.

"Don't start, Wash," Colonel Duncan warned. "I'm in a foul mood to hear excuses."

They gathered around a small campfire and enjoyed a fine supper cooked up by Doc Trimble. Generous slices of a savory roast near filled the tin plates, followed by potatoes and carrots so tender they came apart on a fork. To top it off, Doc had baked a peach cobbler. After stuffing himself, Jake wondered if he would be able to get atop a horse to ride evening watch.

"Looks like Doc'll have us all fattened up before long," Josh boasted as he collected plates.

"He's done right by us, hasn't he?" Ty Wells asked as he refilled his coffee cup.

"Here's to the cook, then!" Si called, and the crew gave Trimble a well-deserved howl.

"Don't think you can flatter me into letting you sleep in tomorrow," Trimble told them. There was just a trace of a grin to his mouth, though.

Jake had mounted his relief horse, a pale mustang peppered with dark spots, when a swirl of dust rose from the northwest.

"Colonel!" Jake called.

"I see it," Colonel Duncan replied. "Jake, collect Gene and have a look."

Jake nodded. He then galloped out to where Gene Stuart rode watch over the western fringe of the herd.

"Colonel said to have a look," Jake explained as he pointed to the dust.

"Got your rifle along?" Gene asked.

"No," Jake said, feeling the blood flow out of his legs. "You?"

"Colonel doesn't care much for this outfit standin' guard with guns," Gene explained. "Shots can start a stampede faster'n wildfire."

"Maybe we'll be lucky," Jake said as he led the way west.

"Sure," Gene agreed. "They could be poor thieves."

"Long as they're not Kiowa or Comanche," Jake muttered. "I don't much care for the notion of getting myself sliced into slivers."

"Nope," Gene said, shuddering. "Buzzards can cut me up themselves. Don't need any help."

They rode a half mile before spying three riders driving forty reluctant steers toward the Duncan herd. Clearly the animals were the missing strays. As for the riders, Jake saw nothing to allay his fears. The two on either side were young—certainly not yet out of their teens. They wore farmers' overalls and crude rawhide hats. The one in the center was different, though. He had to be thirty, thirty-five even. Long sandy-blond hair emerged from under a black beaver hat. He rode with a measured gait, and his eyes were cold and hard—killer's eyes. He wore a pistol on each hip, and his clothes were cut so that they blended with each curve and angle of his body.

"Range thieves?" Jake asked.

"I don't think so," Gene said, riding out so the approaching riders could see him. "That middle one—"

His words were cut short by a shout from the far side of

the herd. The two boys pinched in the herd so that the animals formed a narrow column. While they drove the strays past Gene and along toward the Duncan herd, the hard-eyed gunman turned to meet Gene.

Jake swallowed hard and nudged his mustang toward Gene. Maybe the stranger would hesitate if he thought others were nearby.

"It's all right," Gene declared as Jake nudged his mustang alongside. "I recognize him now."

"What?" Jake cried.

"It's Lofland," Gene explained. "Grew impatient, most likely."

Jake tried to control his nervous fingers as Stan Lofland approached. It wasn't possible. The gunman had acquired a well-deserved reputation as a dangerous man, and his gaze was enough to unsettle anybody.

"Thought you'd join us in Sherman," Gene declared as Lofland slowed his horse.

"Figure you'll have a herd when you get there?" Lofland asked.

"Maybe," Gene replied. "Got a shirker ridin' left point."

"That better change," Lofland said, spitting stale tobacco juice off to the side. "I was riding down to have a look over the trail when I happened across these two boys, driving Bar JD steers south. Seems the colonel offered 'em work."

"They got an early start, it appears," Gene observed. "It's a good thing. The colonel's none too happy over those strays."

"How come him to put a weak man on point?" Lofland asked as he motioned toward the herd.

"He's got his fool nephew along," Gene explained.

"Wash?" Lofland asked, spitting again. "Well, that explains plenty. This youngster the one let the cows run off?"

Jake flinched as Lofland's heavy gaze fell onto him.

"No, this here's Jake Wetherby," Gene explained. "He's reliable enough. He and I stopped the whole herd from swingin' west."

"Who's the fellow I should talk to, then?" Lofland asked.

"Nobody," Gene said, avoiding Lofland's eyes. "You talk it over with Colonel Duncan, Mr. Lofland. I expect he'll let bygones be, what with the strays returned and all."

"Maybe," Lofland muttered. "Maybe not. Either way, it best not happen a second time."

Jake was more than a little glad when they arrived at the camp. He quickly turned the mustang and rode out to his guard station. Even from a distance he could hear arguing in the camp. A few minutes later Jordy rode out to join him.

"You don't have watch till nightfall," Jake told his brother.

"I know," Jordy said, staring uneasily back toward the camp. "I don't know I feel too easy back there, though. This new man, Lofland, had words with Wash."

"Lofland's no man to tangle with," Jake noted.

"I figured that real quick," Jordy replied. "Seems to me everybody ought to be glad the strays are back, but instead they're barking at each other like a pack of wild dogs."

"Well, maybe some good'll come of it," Jake remarked. "Colonel Duncan needs to deal with Wash and that Albert fellow."

"If he doesn't, I figure Lofland will."

"Wish I could find comfort in the notion," Jake said, frowning. "I can't help wondering what'll happen if I'm the next one to make a mistake."

"Or if I am, huh?"

"Yeah," Jake confessed. "Or Josh."

If Lofland's arrival unsettled the crew, the other newcomers proved to be more welcome. Len Baxter and Oliver Phipps were Grayson County orphans, cousins on their mother's side, and more like brothers in Jake's estimation.

Len was a quick-witted seventeen-year-old with dark brown hair and a talent for spinning yarns. Ollie was only fifteen. Three inches shy of Jordy's height, Ollie had bare shoulders as bony as Josh's. He rode as if born on horseback, though, and he amused his companions by strumming a guitar and singing in a sweet, somewhat too solemn voice the most outrageously bawdy tunes imaginable.

"Made his living last winter in a Fort Worth saloon,"

Len explained. "Picked up too many bad habits. I do believe he swore those fool longhorns back here faster than a dozen men with bullwhips could've managed it. And I warn you here and now. Lock your sisters up 'fore he gets a look at 'em.''

Jake judged young Phipps a milder case by far. Ollie rapidly settled into the company. That first night he was showing Jericho a few guitar chords, and he managed to pair himself nicely with Jordy and Tip during night watch.

After proving their merit that next day on the trail north, John Duncan assigned them to take charge of the herd's right flank. That allowed Ron Callahan to move up to left point, a decision that satisfied everyone but Martin Albert.

"Your uncle's not much for giving a man a second chance, is he?" Albert asked Wash when the two of them spread their blankets beside the cook wagon two days later. "I won't ride drag with those children, coughing out my lungs and getting spattered with horse dung!"

"I'll see you're moved up front again," Wash promised.

Jake was sitting with Josh, helping move supplies around the wagon, and he fought to hold back a curse.

"Doc says that Albert won't make it halfway," Josh whispered. "Either Lofland'll kill him or the colonel will pay him off."

"Don't bet on it, Peanut," Jake grumbled. "Bad pennies have a way of hanging around. It's never as easy to get rid of 'em as it should be."

Indeed it wasn't. Next morning, when Wash urged his uncle to reassign Albert, John Duncan could barely restrain his anger.

"You want him to ride up front with us?" the colonel cried.

"He isn't much use riding drag," Lofland noted. "But at least back there a body on horseback serves to hurry the cows along. Here I'm swallowing dust and baking myself on the left flank, and I don't complain."

"Maybe you ought to mount Josh there and turn the wash bucket over to Albert," Callahan suggested.

Josh had the misfortune to be nearby, refilling coffee cups, when Albert jumped to his feet. Josh tried to hop clear, but Albert's left arm dislodged the coffeepot, and scalding liquid spattered the ill-tempered fellow's legs.

"Little fool!" Albert shouted, kicking Josh hard in the thigh and knocking the boy into a wagon wheel.

"Hold on," Eddie urged as Jake threw his plate aside.

"Jake?" Jordy asked as he reached for a large rock.

"I'm all right," Josh declared, stumbling to his feet.

"Clumsy fool," Albert growled. "Better learn to be more careful."

"Good advice," Doc muttered as he hobbled over to pick up the coffeepot. "For lots of men."

Jake felt his face flash red, but Josh gave him a pleading glance.

"It's for him to settle," Eddie whispered.

"He's my brother," Jake insisted.

"You want him to be a cook's boy all his life?" Eddie asked.

Jake shook his head, and Eddie forced a grin.

"Then give him leave to fight his own battles," Eddie urged. "If he doesn't square things, we'll happen by the fool when he has night watch tomorrow."

Jake glared at Albert, but he held himself in check. And as it turned out, Eddie had been right. Josh had his revenge that very night.

Exactly how or when he managed it, Jake never was altogether certain. It seemed to all of them Josh was busy from dawn to dusk, and the crew's bedding was stowed away all that time. Even so, once supper was concluded and night watch mounted, Martin Albert shed his britches, rolled out his blankets, and took to his bed. He hardly touched his bare legs to the blankets before he jumped up, howling and thrashing about like a wild man.

"Ayyyy!" he screamed as he fought to pry something from his legs.

"Lord a'mighty!" Ron Callahan exclaimed, fighting off a

howl of laughter. "You've gone and laid down in a patch of prickly pear!"

"I did not!" Albert insisted as he plucked a spiny green disk from one leg. "Somebody's messed with my bed!"

"Now who'd do a thing like that?" Doc Trimble asked as he hobbled over with a small cup of reddish ointment. "Good thing we prepared this medicine, eh, Josh?"

"Sure was," Josh said, grinning from ear to ear.

Albert took a step toward his young tormentor, but Stan Lofland interceded.

"You got something to say, do you?" Lofland asked.

"I still have some cactus stuck to me," Albert said, retreating.

"Why didn't you say so?" Lofland replied with a grin. He then stepped over and none too gently tore prickly pear from Albert's legs and hindquarters.

"Fetch my tweezers, Josh," Doc Trimble then instructed as he waved Albert over near the fire. "This may hurt some, young fellow, and the ointment's apt to burn a hair."

"I'll—" Albert started to say, but his words were drowned in a howl when Doc pulled out the first of several embedded spines.

"Always a good idea to check your blankets before you hop into 'em," Ty observed as Albert winced and groaned.

"Sure is," Lofland agreed. "You're apt to remember this night when you put your rump in the saddle tomorrow."

"You don't expect me to—" Albert began.

"That or I pay you off," Colonel Duncan said, stepping over. "Paint him up real pretty, Doc. Josh, you think you can find me some hot coffee? Seems like there's a chill to the wind tonight."

It must have been hot enough to melt butter, and Jake couldn't help laughing. The others joined in, and Ollie made up a thinly veiled dinty to celebrate Josh's revenge.

"I have a long memory, boy," Albert warned Josh afterward.

"Yeah?" Jake asked. "Then you'll remember he's got

brothers, won't you? Doesn't seem to me that a few cactus spines was much trouble.''

"Sure doesn't," Eddie added. "Nothin' at all."

Albert sat there, glaring, for half an hour, though.

7

Gradually Jake settled into the routine of the trail drive. Whether atop Maizy or the peppery-colored mustang, he grew to be one with his mount. Cutting off strays or turning the herd back toward the road became second nature. But while he and the other cowboys were adjusting to the cattle, the herd was still a long way from trail-broken.

"Fool longhorns never do quite settle down, do they?" Jordy asked when he and Jake rode night watch together. "You'd almost suspect they know what's waiting for them at trail's end."

"You figure they do?" Jake asked.

"Sure would explain a lot," Jordy declared. " 'Course, considering what we've already done to 'em, they don't have too many reasons to look on us kindly."

Jake laughed at the notion. Still, there were times when he swore to himself the longhorns held a particular grudge against cowboys, and Jake Wetherby in particular.

Ten miles south of Preston, as Jake was about to surrender his watch to Ron Callahan, the longhorns began to stir. First the animals on the far left began groaning and stomping around. Then Maizy, too, grew restless.

"What is it, girl?" Jake whispered.

The mare snorted at the wind, and Jake turned toward a low tree-studded rise a quarter mile away. An eerie howl flooded the air, and the cattle began to move off.

"Wolf, huh?" Jake muttered. "I guess these cows think it's hungry for fresh ribs."

Jordy and Ollie had the far flank, and they took up a calm-

53

ing lullaby. It helped some, but as long as that wolf went on howling, the herd wasn't going to rest.

"What's the trouble?" Eddie asked as he arrived with the relief watch.

"Wolf," Jake explained. "I guess we'll have to ride out and shoot the fool critter."

"I don't take with shootin' wolves," Si argued. "Not when the moon's full. That's the worst sort of bad luck."

"You and your superstitions," Jake grumbled.

"I never heard of any curse to go with shootin' wolves," Eddie remarked, "but nobody's shootin' off a rifle tonight. The herd's already nervous, and a shot would set 'em to runnin'."

"Then what do we do?" Jake asked.

"Rouse the others," Eddie explained. "Looks like the whole outfit's losin' sleep this night."

It proved a trying night, especially for those on early watch. The others got a nod or two of sleep. Jake greeted the morning with red-streaked eyes. His rump was numb from riding, and except for a brief pause to eat breakfast, he didn't get one ounce of rest.

"Uncle John, we're all wore out," Wash announced as Doc Trimble began packing up the wagon. "We ought to lay over, rest up."

"Figure that wolf'll head off yonder?" Eddie asked. "No, we need to get clear of here."

"But the men—" Wash objected.

"Will start earning their keep!" the colonel barked. "From time to time I'll pull a man off and let him get some rest in the cook wagon."

"Mostly we'll just doze a hair as we ride," Callahan added. "Only watch out you don't let the steers know. They can turn on a dozin' man quick."

"Keep an eye on the men ahead and behind you," Colonel Duncan advised. "Anybody starts to drift, ride out and rouse him."

Gene Stuart rode up and shook Jake to life twice before midday.

"You best take a turn at the wagon, Jake," Gene advised. "You're nigh dead."

None of their humors improved when the wind suddenly shifted. Clouds appeared overhead, choking the sun with their threatening shades of gray-black. The wind howled out of the north, sending icy shivers up Jake's side.

"It's almost June!" Jake shouted to the screaming wind. "No time for a norther!"

Texas weather had a bad habit of surprising a man, though, and it wasn't put off by a cowboy's shouts and curses. The air grew colder by the moment, and it took every ounce of coaxing Jake possessed to convince the herd to continue. That sharp wind tormented the longhorns, stinging their faces and chilling their insides.

"Ain't doin' much for us cowboys, either!" Gene declared when he brought Jake a blanket from the cook wagon. "Wrap it around you 'fore you sprout icicles from your nose."

Actually, there were other parts of him far colder.

"Yeah, I know," Gene said, laughing. "Not much helpin' those parts. Would you believe it? I got a fine new set of flannel drawers back at the station. Left 'em with Miz Miranda."

"Flannel'd be nice," Jake said, shivering. "I just wish my homespuns didn't have so many holes in 'em."

"Yeah," Gene said, managing a chuckle between chattering teeth. "I got similar troubles."

Jake hoped and prayed for better weather, but instead it turned worse. Cold sheets of rain began to lash out at them, and in no time the whole outfit was soaked to the skin. Jake had brought an oilskin poncho along, but he was wet before he had a chance to throw it over him, and even then, rain managed to find every seam.

"We can't go on this way," Jake lamented as the cattle sloshed their way north along the muddy remains of the Preston Road.

Jake wasn't the only one to come to that conclusion. By and by Colonel Duncan rode by with a pale-faced Wash.

"How far's it to Preston?" Jake asked.

"Still better than five miles away," the colonel explained. "No hope of getting there tonight. The herd's bogging down, and I read thunder in those clouds. We get a good boom or two, and the whole bunch's bound to run."

"So what do we do?" Jake asked.

"There's a rise of ground up ahead with creeks on three sides," Colonel Duncan explained. "Turn the herd north and leave them to wander on by themselves. They won't get across that creek bed, not with all this rain. You move back and help Gene contain the flank."

"Yes, sir," Jake said, blinking droplets from his eyes.

"Wish we could turn toward Sherman and find a dry barn for the men," the colonel continued, "but we'd lose too much time."

"Sure," Jake agreed. "This rain can't last forever."

But as it continued to torment man and beast, Jake grew less certain. He, Jordy, Jer, and Si made a shelter of sorts by draping their ponchos across a framework of cottonwood limbs, and that kept the worst of the rain off long enough for each to find some sleep. The ground was cold and soggy, though, and Jake awoke chilled through. Ollie and Len had been the only smart ones. They erected their shelter in the low branches of a live oak.

"We're Grayson County boys, remember?" Len boasted when the sun finally broke through the clouds that next morning. "You'd expect us to know what to do."

Jake's sole consolation had been knowing Josh would sleep in the wagon with Doc Trimble, but the youngster looked like a wet rag when he dished out breakfast.

"What happened to you, Peanut?" Jake cried.

"Wagon spring a leak?" Jordy added.

"Got moved out," Josh explained, coughing. "Doc and I bedded down in the cottonwoods."

"Moved out?" Jake asked, eyeing Martin Albert in particular.

"Not for him, at least," Josh whispered. "Lofland."

"Albert looks mighty dry, though," Jake noted.

"I think he and Wash rode into Sherman when they had watch," Josh said quietly. "They got whiskey on their breath."

Jake felt his dander rise, and he kicked a small stone toward Albert. Eddie hurried over and led Jake aside.

"Don't get riled," Eddie urged. "Gene and I had the same watch. We saw to it the herd stayed quiet."

"It was their—" Jake began.

"Now, what good were they doin', huh?" Eddie asked. "Likely did us all a favor leavin'. You got to know by now they won't pull their load. I been on outfits where the boss had his kin along before. They generally prove a disappointment."

"We can't go on letting them do this," Jake argued.

"It's not my job, and it sure as thunder ain't yours, Jake, to run this drive. Mind your own responsibilities and leave the colonel to handle his nephew."

Jake frowned. He was wet and cold, tired and angry. For two bits he would have laid into Martin Albert and Wash Duncan, the both of them. But Eddie was right. What would it change? Instead he accepted a steaming cup of coffee from Josh and tried to shake himself warm.

Jake would have welcomed a day's rest, but John Duncan ordered the men out to their stations once breakfast was eaten. Doc Trimble did hang wet clothing from ropes on the cook wagon, and the sun rose, promising fairer weather.

"We're a real sight today, eh?" Jordy asked when he saddled his horse.

Jake had to grin his agreement. The whole crew had stripped down to trousers or drawers, allowing their clothes to dry, and little Ollie Phipps galloped by in an oversized nightshirt.

"Now there's a sight to remember!" Gene declared, laughing so hard he half fell off his horse.

Wet clothes were nothing compared to wet saddles and blankets, though. Jake knew the horses would suffer considerably, and he wasn't the only one to swap mounts frequently as they drove the herd on toward Preston.

Once they neared the Red River, the landscape began to change. There were sharper edges to the hills, and the gullies were broader, with steep sides. Farmhouses sprouted alongside the road, too, and children sometimes sat atop fence rails, waving as the herd rumbled past.

"I hope for modesty's sake those clothes dry quick," Gene told Jake when they passed a pair of attractive girls. "I feel plum naked."

"Maybe Ollie can spare you his nightshirt," Jake suggested, grinning.

"That wouldn't help too much," Gene replied. "It's got too many holes in the back. Poor Ollie must feel properly ventilated."

By midday, wind and sun had dried out most of the clothes, but the men didn't hurry to fetch them. The trail had turned dusty dry, and where they would have welcomed the heat a day before, it now turned oppressive. Jake coughed as dust clung to his perspiring flesh and tormented his throat. His hair was fast turning sticky gray. With farms on both sides of the trail, they had to narrow the herd, too, and that meant riding even closer to the animals and chewing that strange mixture of dust and dung the longhorns sent swirling into the air.

Colonel Duncan set off ahead to secure supplies from the small trading post Holland Coffee operated on the river. Eddie, meanwhile, swung the herd out toward Rock Bluff Crossing.

"Here's where we start earnin' our pay!" Gene declared as he motioned toward the ribbon of water cutting its way through a wide bottomland of treacherous red earth.

"Looks like quicksand," Jake observed.

"Is, most of it," Gene replied. "Trick's to cut a path for men and cows that won't swallow both."

It didn't seem promising. What was worse, once Colonel Duncan secured supplies, he sent Doc Trimble's wagon to Preston to collect them.

"Be a cold supper tonight," Eddie observed as the men

made camp on a rise overlooking the river. "Dry beef to chew for breakfast."

"Why?" Jake asked.

"The wagon will head on east to Colbert's ferry," Eddie explained. "Can't risk losin' it in the bog."

"Our bedding's in there," Ty complained.

"Guess we'll have a night to pass on hard ground, huh?" Jordy asked.

"At least it ain't still rainin'," Ollie remarked as he untied his guitar from behind his saddle.

"Not just this moment," Ty grumbled, eyeing a threatening line of clouds to the north.

"Ah, it's a cowboy's life," Ollie insisted, laughing as he strummed his guitar.

"Whatever happened to the adventure anyway, Jake?" Jordy whispered.

"To tell you the truth, I'm having about all the adventure I can handle just now," Jake replied.

Fortunately, Colonel Duncan had allowed a coffeepot at the camp, so as evening crept closer, there was steaming liquid to chase off the twilight chill. Len shared a tale of murderous Indians, and Ollie entertained them with an original tune.

> "Lonesome trails, I've been ridin'
> Never thought from honest work I'd be hidin'.
> Heat and dusk, cold and rain—
> All in all, I believe, it's mostly pain.
> The Shawnee Trail ain't for the weak hearts.
> No, it's partial hard on all your tender parts."

It wasn't the best melody Jake had ever heard, but the words pretty well captured their feelings. As Jordy said afterward, "I feel rubbed raw, beat down, and stomped on."

"And this is the easy part of the trip," Gene observed. "Wait till we get across Red River and start north. There you got Indians and murderers to worry over."

"First you got to cross, though," Eddie warned. "There's easier things to get done."

The words were prophecy. Jake felt himself shook awake an hour shy of dawn that next morning.

"Sleep better?" Eddie whispered.

"Well enough," Jake replied, yawning. "Not long enough, though."

"Well, Colonel Duncan's given us a genuine challenge," Eddie explained. "Seems there's no scout hereabouts to mark the crossin', so you and I get the task."

"I don't know anything about river crossings," Jake objected. "And I've only crossed the Red River once in my whole life. That was hundreds of miles farther east, too."

"All you got to do's hold the markin' sticks," Eddie explained, motioning to a stack of blackjack oak limbs with small scraps of red cloth tied to one end.

"I suppose I can manage that."

"Better, since you don't really have a choice," Eddie said, grinning. "Come on. This gets us out of night watch tomorrow."

That promise was all the encouragement Jake needed. He shook himself to life, pulled on his trousers, and hurried to saddle Maizy. In no time he was tying the bundle of sticks behind his saddle. Then he and Eddie set off down the bank into the boggy river bottom.

8

If Jake had known half as much about quicksand before as he did afterward, he never would have followed Eddie Stuart down the embankment at Rock Bluff and along into the river bottom. The riverbed was a mixture of gummy clay and sand, and it was absolutely impassable in most places. Eddie's horse was nearly sucked right down to his nose once, but Jake managed to toss out a rope, and Eddie got its loop over the horse in time.

"You don't mean to try and drive a herd through this, do you?" Jake cried. "We'll lose 'em all."

"In this? Sure, we will," Eddie agreed. "Trick's to find a place where's there solid ground at the bank and the river beyond is halfway shallow."

For a considerable time Jake thought it unlikely. Finally Eddie managed to slosh his way out into the river proper.

"Bring the sticks!" he shouted. "Mark my trail."

Jake nudged Maizy ahead. With a fair degree of caution, he dismounted and embedded a stake in the indentations left by Eddie's horse. Every five feet or so a red cloth rustled in the morning breeze, until Jake was in the river itself. He then splashed his way downstream to where Eddie had emerged on hard, rocky ground.

"Now, we have to see how wide the crossing is," Eddie explained as he turned eastward. He repeated his march down the river and on across toward Rock Bluff. Then he and Jake marked the crossing and inspected it a second time.

"Won't be easy, controlling the herd," Jake observed.

"You've got a route a hundred feet wide, and you expect to run a thousand longhorns through it."

"Small batches at a time," Eddie explained.

"I've seen steers in water before," Jake warned. "They get to thrashing about, and a man on horseback's awful vulnerable."

"Sure, he is," Eddie agreed. "He has to be mighty watchful. But there's no other way to get it done. We got the crossin' marked. Now it's time to fetch the colonel."

Of all the perils lurking on a cattle trail, river crossings stood near the top of anybody's list. If Jake hadn't known that already, all he had to do was scan the faces of the experienced hands to get confirmation. Colonel Duncan took great care to place reliable hands in the vanguard and on the flanks, leaving the easier task of urging the cattle across the river to the newcomers. Jake had driven longhorns across the Brazos and the Trinity, but those rivers were rivulets compared to the Red River.

"Be easier if we hadn't had so much rain the other day," Jake grumbled as he took his place alongside Gene Stuart.

"No, it's ten times worse in late summer," Gene told him. "The dryer the river, the worse the quicksand. It may seem like you're on solid ground. Then the bottom reaches up and snags you."

"You sure?" Jake asked. "Seems like it'd be the other way around."

"I've seen it, Jake," Gene insisted. "Have you?"

Thereafter, Jake kept his observations to himself. He recalled something his grandfather had once said.

"Son, you know just enough to be dangerous."

With brothers and friends counting on him, Jake didn't intend to make a mistake.

Ron Callahan and Ty Wells stayed up on the bank with Jordy and Tip Stuart. Their job was to mind the main body as the others cut off a hundred head at a time to drive across the river. Jake and Gene held the right flank while Len and Ollie watched the left. Eddie and Colonel Duncan, together with Wash and Martin Albert, led the first animals across.

Jericho and Si shouted and waved rope ends in an effort to urge the stragglers along.

The crossing went well at first. Half the animals got across without mishap. Then a cow broke a leg, and a pair of steers strayed downstream and were carried off in the current.

"Watch 'em, Wash!" the colonel shouted as he waved his nephew toward the trouble spot.

Wash rode down among the steers and threw a rope around one in danger of foundering. With Albert's help, Wash dragged the beast across to dry land.

Two more longhorns drowned when the sixth batch started across, but the next groups fared better. Then, just as Jake was beginning to relax, seven steers broke away and tried to escape along the treacherous bank.

"I got 'em," Jericho hollered as he turned his horse and cut them off. The steers tried a second route, but Ollie splashed over and shouted the animals on across the river.

"Calm 'em down, boys!" the colonel urged.

"Sing 'em a song, Ollie," Len suggested.

"Wild women, wild women," Ollie began, brushing a tangle of blond hair back from his eyes. "Can't wait till I get me some more o' them wild women!"

Jake wasn't quite sure what set the cattle off. He doubted it was Ollie's singing. More likely it was the way the wind caught Ollie's oversized nightshirt. The boy seemed more ghost than cowboy, and longhorns were prone to spooking.

Whatever started it, the whole batch turned in a flash and surged toward Ollie and Jericho. Beyond was a deep pool, and soon the two youngsters found themselves struggling to keep atop their mounts. The horses, screaming furiously as the river of horns grew closer, escaped, leaving their riders frantically thrashing toward where a cottonwood branch stretched out over the river.

"Hold on, Jer!" Si shouted as he tried to turn the cattle. Jake was charging down the bank in an effort to do the same. John Duncan managed to draw a pistol and fire into the river before either got near the stranded boys.

The shot had an instantaneous effect. The noise turned the

longhorns back toward the bank. As for the ones already on the north side, it sent them running.

"Ayyyy!" Si shouted as he charged the last reluctant animals and chased them on across the river. Jake then splashed his way into the roiling water and made his way to the cottonwood.

"Best take your brother there first," Ollie sputtered when Jake pulled Maizy alongside. "He's half drowned."

"Jer!" Jake shouted.

Jericho managed a faint nod. With Ollie's help, Jake pulled his brother up behind him and rode back to the south bank. By that time Si had regained solid ground, too, and he took charge of his old friend.

"Ollie!" Len suddenly shouted.

Jake turned and stared in horror as the cottonwood began to shudder. The mass of cattle thundering along the north bank had loosened its roots.

"I'm coming!" Jake shouted as he turned back toward the river.

Ollie glanced at the tree, gazed out at the distance separating him from his rescuers, and smiled faintly.

"Wild women!" he bellowed as he tried to jump away from the tree. His foot caught in a forked branch, though, and when the tree broke loose, it pushed him under as it was swept downstream.

"Ollie!" Len screamed helplessly as the cottonwood floated beyond his outstretched arms.

"No!" Jake howled as Maizy fought his efforts to pursue.

It happened just that quickly. One minute Ollie stood there wailing away. The next he was gone. Colonel Duncan splashed back to the south bank and suggested Len ride down and have a look downstream.

"You can never tell," the colonel said sourly. "That tree might turn. Boy could be sitting up on the bank, laughing."

"I suspect not, Colonel," Len said, frowning.

"I'll go with you," Jake offered.

"Sure," Len said, gazing back at where Jericho sat, coughing up muddy water. "Glad of the company."

They rode up to the bluff and followed the river a half mile to where it made a turn. There, on a narrow sandbar, the cottonwood came to a rest. Nearby was an odd white mound.

"It's him," Len said, leading the way down the bluff.

Jake followed as best he could on a weary horse. He wasn't eager to get there. He didn't detect any movement from Ollie, and he never had taken death very well.

When Jake finally splashed onto the sandbar, he saw Len sitting in the shallows, cradling his cousin's body. River rocks and tree branches had stripped Ollie's shirt and torn the flesh on his right side. His face remained unmarked, though, and his cold eyes gazed up with a mixture of calm and surprise.

"He's dead," Len announced matter-of-factly. "Fool boy! Never did learn to swim."

"He let me take Jer first," Jake mumbled as he dismounted.

"Wasn't just bein' kindhearted about that," Len declared. "He was scairt to let go."

"He looks so little there. Just a kid."

"We ain't any of us very old," Len said, gazing up with swollen eyes. "He's got brothers even littler farmed off to folks here and there. I should've left Ollie to do the same, only he was such good company."

"He was that," Jake agreed as he helped hoist the corpse up onto Maizy's back. Len was reluctant to let go of his burden, but Jake pointed to the herd.

"Sure," Len muttered. "We've got work waitin'."

"We'll find a good spot for him up on the bluff," Jake promised. "Where he can watch the sun rise and set."

"Wish it was a churchyard," Len said, sighing. "Out back of a saloon even. Someplace where there'd be music sometimes."

"Yeah," Jake agreed. "That would be a fine notion. We'll come by and sing for him sometimes."

"Sure, we will," Len agreed, swallowing hard.

"Be too quiet in camp tonight," Jake muttered.

"Tonight, tomorrow night, and a lot more nights after that," Len noted.

The rest of the herd was brought across the Red River without incident. By then the Stuart brothers had headed off the runaways, and the entire herd was grouped on the north bank.

Doc Trimble and Josh arrived in time to cook supper, and the whole outfit seemed to brighten a hair at the notion of something hot inside.

Jericho walked off with Len, and Jake worried some about it. They returned just before supper with a couple of fresh-hewn oak boards. One of them bore a neatly carved guitar with an inscription underneath.

Oliver Aaron Phipps
1843–1857
R. I. P.

"You got the dates wrong," Jordy said, staring hard at the boards. "He was fifteen."

"No, a hair shy of fourteen, to be truthful," Len explained as he set the boards behind the wagon. A few feet away little Ollie lay wrapped in a weathered quilt his mother had made. The youngster had preferred it to blankets.

"Len says he liked to stretch the truth," Jericho explained. "Stretch himself, too, I guess. It would've been me there if he hadn't helped me onto Jake's horse."

"Wasn't your doin', Jer," Len insisted. "Just the way it is out here."

Maybe it was, Jake told himself, but Ollie's death turned the whole camp solemn. That night Jericho was tormented by one nightmare after another, and Jake wasn't the only one who awoke earlier than usual to find himself lying in blankets damp with cold sweat.

He and Jericho dug a trench atop a rise overlooking Rock Bluff Crossing, and the whole outfit gathered for the burial. Colonel Duncan quoted scripture, and Ty Wells recited a hymn. Then Len opened the quilt so they could peer down at Ollie's young face a final time.

"He was a good hand," Colonel Duncan declared. "We'll miss his singing in particular."

"I looked forward to watchin' him at trail's end," Tip said, grinning. "If he was half as handy with gals as he boasted—"

"He never even led one out walkin'," Len admitted. "Liked to talk about it 'cause it troubled him some. He wasn't but a little nub of a boy, you see, but he had grand thoughts."

"You had a mighty short ride, little Ollie, but it had its moments," Eddie said, gently folding the quilt's corner back over Ollie's face.

Each man lent a hand, and they lowered their young companion into the red earth together. Then Jericho brought the youngster's guitar over and prepared to set it on Ollie's chest.

"No, that would never do," Len said, shaking his head. "You remember how the two of you passed those first few nights outside of Sherman, scratchin' out tunes?"

"I remember," Jericho replied. "I always will."

"Ollie told me to make sure if anything happened to him, you took that guitar and made music with it," Len explained. "He wouldn't want the music to stop just 'cause he can't play anymore."

"I can't take it," Jericho argued, passing the guitar toward Len. "Don't you see, Lenny? I'm the one got him killed!"

"No, that was just bad luck," Len said, grabbing Jericho's hand and holding onto him a moment. "Ollie never had many breaks in his life, but he never held a grudge against anybody. Sure wouldn't think ill of you, Jer. You two were friends. Take that guitar. When you play it, sing to the wind. Maybe it'll whisper along out here where Ollie can hear."

"Think so, Jake?" Jericho asked.

"Hope so," Jake replied. "I know I'll rest easier thinking it's so."

They then shoveled dirt over Ollie's pitiful remains and covered the mound with rocks to keep animals away. Afterward Len and Jericho set the head- and footboards in place.

"Isn't anything left for us to do here," Colonel Duncan

finally announced. "We've paid a price to get across the river into the Indian Nations. Let's be sure we didn't pay it for nothing."

"Time to head north," Eddie announced.

"Let's ride," Gene added.

Jake gave Jericho an understanding nod and left him with Si. Moments later Jake was heaving a saddle onto Maizy's back. The dead were, after all, buried. It was time for the living to get on with their labors.

9

Colonel Duncan led the way north from the Red River along a branch river that wound its way to the northwest.

"This is the Washita," the colonel told Jake when he pulled alongside. "I've been told it means buffalo, but I can't be sure of it. An Indian's apt to tell a white man anything and laugh at the way he laps it up."

"We're in Indian country now, aren't we?" Jake asked.

"Land of the Chickasaw."

"Don't you figure we ought to arm ourselves, Colonel? After all the trouble we had with Comanches and Kiowas on the Brazos, I wouldn't care to be caught helpless."

"Not likely to face Kiowas here," Duncan argued. "There's an army fort a little less than twenty miles to the north, and the Chickasaws hereabouts are a long time past raiding. Truth is, whites are more trouble in the Nations. They aren't any too mindful of the law, and the trail to St. Louis has become a bandit's hunting ground."

"Then we ought to have our rifles with us," Jake complained.

"Lofland's got his weapons," Colonel Duncan noted. "He'll know when there's need of firing. You youngsters are far too likely to pull out your rifles, shoot at shadows, and start the cattle running."

"I'm a long time past being a youngster, Colonel," Jake argued. "And there are a thousand longhorns between me and Lofland."

"I'm here, though, Jacob Henry. And before trouble gets a toehold, I promise you we'll all of us be armed."

Jake tried to take comfort in the colonel's confident nod, but that hadn't kept Ollie Phipps from drowning, and it wouldn't bend the path of a Kiowa lance.

South of the Red River, Jake knew they would have covered the fifteen miles to the army post at Fort Washita in a single day. There was good grass north of Rock Bluff Crossing, though, and three different times Colonel Duncan ordered the herd halted.

"Doesn't do any good to drive skeletons to St. Louis," Gene Stuart told Jake. "There are places where the land on either side of the trail's held by ranchers and farmers. You graze your herd there, and it costs."

As it turned out, resting the herd on the banks of the Washita had its cost as well. As the men wearily rolled off their horses near the camp Doc Trimble and Josh had made on a hill overlooking the river, a band of riders approached from the east.

"Time for the rifles, Colonel?" Jake asked.

"Not this time," Lofland announced.

"Toll collectors," Eddie explained. "Gettin' it done early this trip."

Jake didn't understand at first, but he caught on once the riders reached the camp. Their leader, a brown-faced man of forty wearing three turkey feathers in a beaver hat, introduced himself as the representative of the Chickasaw tribe.

"This is our land," he declared. "We didn't invite your cows to come and chew our grass."

"We don't plan to stay past morning," Colonel Duncan explained. "We're bound for Fort Washita, and from there north to St. Louis."

"You'll be a week on tribal land, then," the Chickasaw grumbled. "I'll want four bits a head toll for grazing our lands."

"You value your grass, don't you?" Wash said, frowning. "We look like rich men to you?"

"I'm sorry," the colonel said, motioning Wash away. "My nephew's excitable. He doesn't understand the way things are done. Climb down and join us for a bit. I'm certain we can resolve the matter peacefully.''

"Sure, we can," Lofland added, stepping to Colonel Duncan's side. The Chickasaws noted the twin pistols and agreed to talk.

To start with, John Duncan introduced himself, Lofland, and the others seated around the cook fire. The Chickasaws reacted to the colonel's name with a nod, but they sat up and took notice at the mention of Stan Lofland.

"I'm Charlie Berry," the Chickasaw leader explained. "You talk like you've been north before."

"I keep a freight station down in Texas," the colonel explained. "I've been to St. Louis on the stagecoach. This is our first herd to bring up the Shawnee Trail, but I've driven cattle elsewhere. And I've heard of the tribes collecting tolls."

"You eat our grass and drink our rivers," Berry said, motioning toward the herd. "I figure it's only fair."

"I won't say it isn't," Colonel Duncan responded. "But fifty cents a head? I didn't pay that much for full-grown beeves back south."

"You ain't in Texas now," Berry pointed out.

"Nevertheless, I won't be robbed," Duncan insisted. "Reconsider, won't you?"

"I've got a hundred men that'll ride down here and help change your mind," Berry warned.

"You wouldn't want a fight," Lofland replied, sliding a pistol out of its holster. "Money's not worth dying for. Not when all you have to do is be reasonable."

"Such as?" Berry asked.

"Why, just lower your asking price," Duncan suggested. "I know your people've known better times. I'll offer you a hundred dollars passage money."

"Ten cents a head?" Berry gasped.

"Easy profit," Lofland noted.

"Fair, too," the colonel argued. "We won't be here but a few days. Like as not, we'll leave some strays behind, so you'll profit from that, too."

"Hundred and fifty," Berry countered.

"Too much," Duncan insisted. "A hundred's fair."

"You ask me to drop my toll four hundred, but you won't sweeten your offer by even fifty dollars?" Berry asked. "I don't believe you put much value in your company. You'll be burying some other boys alongside that one back at the river."

"If you know about that," Duncan declared, "then you know we've already paid a fearful price. We aren't the sort you want to press too hard. And that's what you're doing."

For a few moments Colonel Duncan and Berry stared hard at each other. Neither flinched. Finally Berry shrugged his shoulders and rose.

"Fifty dollars ain't worth fighting over," Berry muttered. "You pay the hundred, and we'll consider ourselves paid."

"Fifty now," Duncan said, pulling out his wallet and drawing out five ten-dollar bank notes. "The rest when we cross Clear Creek four days from now."

"Afraid we might charge you twice, huh?" Berry asked. "We've learned a few white man's tricks, but you'll find my word's good."

"Call me superstitious, then," Duncan urged. "I don't much favor Indian trouble."

"You needn't worry about Chickasaws," Berry assured the colonel. "A party of Kiowas comes through sometimes."

"How would we know the difference?" Wash asked.

"You'll know," Jake declared. "Kiowas got their manner of doing things."

"They'd come at night," Berry explained. "Quiet. Small batches mostly. If you keep alert, they'll keep their distance."

"Thanks for the advice," Duncan said, rising. "I guess now that we've concluded our business, you'll be going."

"Be looking for you at Clear Creek," Berry said as he and his companions turned to go. "Don't go spending our other fifty, now."

"Wouldn't dream of it," Duncan assured them.

After the Chickasaws departed, Wash stepped over to the fire, filled his coffee cup, and mumbled a curse at the Indians.

"No better than road agents," Wash grumbled. "They'll want more than fifty at Clear Creek, Uncle John."

"They won't," Colonel Duncan insisted. "No, we'll be on Choctaw land then."

"And they'll want to be paid, too, huh?" Wash asked.

"Don't you figure they're entitled?" Eddie asked. "This here's their country, after all. You don't think it odd the colonel charges folks who lay over at his station."

"They're not feeding us," Wash complained.

"Feedin' the cows," Eddie pointed out. "Same thing, don't you see? Anyhow, a hundred dollars isn't so much."

"That's because it's not your hundred," Wash replied.

"Nor yours, either," Eddie muttered.

Wash started to take offense, but a sour glance from the colonel froze him. Instead he stalked off past the wagon.

Jake passed the hour before supper resting his weary bones. Long hours in the saddle were breaking down men and animals both, and he vowed to give Maizy a needed day's rest.

After supper, Tip Stuart brought the condition of the remuda to Colonel Duncan's attention.

"Half the horses are breaking down," Tip declared. "I got two ponies with swollen tendons, three with bad shoes, and most all the others have saddle burns."

"Tomorrow we've got a short distance to travel," Duncan noted. "See only the better-rested animals get ridden. We can reduce the night watch, too."

"That'll get us to Fort Washita," Tip said, "but you best see if we can get some remounts there. Or talk with that Chickasaw fellow. Maybe we can trade some with him."

"Horses won't come cheap at Fort Washita," Duncan said, shaking his head. "And I don't want to think about what Berry will ask."

"We talked some about those mustangs when we were still back in Texas, Colonel," Tip said, sighing. "I warrant they've proved out as good enough ridin' horses, but they aren't any of 'em used to constant work."

"Seems you were right about them, son," Duncan admitted. "But that's not going to get us to Missouri. I'll ride ahead tomorrow and try to dicker some with the fort traders. Meanwhile, if you need to, let a hand or two ride in the wagon with Doc."

"Might be a good idea," Tip said, nodding.

Colonel Duncan had the shortage of sound horses in mind when he reduced the night watch. The Washita River blocked the cattle from escaping west or south, too, so a pair of men were posted to the north and another two to the east.

"We'll get some extra sleep tonight, it appears," Gene told Jake. "I'll find it welcome."

"We all will," Jake declared.

The two of them considered themselves doubly fortunate, for John Duncan sent them out on the twilight watch, meaning they would be able to sleep the balance of the night straight through. Jericho and Len Baxter rode along the east rim that same watch, and their soft singing lulled the cattle.

"Once that brother of yours learns how to play Ollie's guitar, he'll be a real pleasure to have around," Gene observed.

"He'll pick it up fast enough," Jake predicted. "He's a fair fiddler already. Learned that real quick."

"I liked little Ollie, but his voice had a way of bitin' at your nerves."

"Was just his voice breaking," Jake said, frowning. "Shame about that boy."

"We'll be downright lucky if he's the only one buried short of Missouri," Gene said, gazing off into the distance. " 'Course, I can think of a couple of fellows I wouldn't much miss."

"Yeah, there's them," Jake agreed. "But they're never the ones."

"No, they're not."

Jake and Gene rode slowly along the peaceful longhorns those next two hours, softly whistling or humming some children's lullaby or church hymn. Jake wished he knew something less solemn, but his hadn't been a family fond of singing. No, Joe Wetherby favored scripture readings when there was any time left when the day's work was done. And except for Jericho fiddling, there hadn't been any music at all.

He found himself remembering those first hard days in Texas. It had been winter then, and he recalled the long nights sharing a room with Jer, Jordy, and Josh—all four of them near frozen as they wriggled beneath one of Grandma Fitch's old cotton quilts.

Jake shivered away a chill. At first he thought it was only the recollection of that winter years before. It wasn't.

"Look up there," Gene said as he pulled his pony alongside.

Jake gazed skyward. A full moon was shining brightly through an odd gray haze. Elsewhere, the millions of sparkling stars were gradually being swallowed by angry black clouds.

"Storm's comin'," Gene said, turning toward the herd.

The cattle, too, sensed the changing weather. Where before they had nestled in the tall buffalo grass, they now stirred restlessly in small groups.

"Best ride into camp," Gene advised. "Warn the colonel."

"You go," Jake urged. "If it comes to it, my horse is sounder."

"That's a pitiful poor argument, Jake," Gene complained.

"Well, think on this, then. I've got a brother yonder."

Gene gazed back to the shadowy figures patrolling the eastern flank and nodded. Jer and Len had resumed their singing, and the longhorns nearest them remained calm.

"Try a tune on 'em yourself," Gene suggested as he turned toward the camp.

"Sure," Jake said, waving Gene along. But in spite of himself, the only song that came to mind was Ollie's crazy tune, "Wild Women." And Jake didn't remember half the words.

Gene had been gone only a minute or so when the first

heavy raindrops pelted Jake's forehead. He quickly dug out his poncho and draped it over his shoulders. The sudden movement upset the cattle, and he was instantly sorry. A dozen started toward him, and it was all he could manage to turn them back. Then a streak of lightning flashed overhead and thunder shook the earth. Instantly the whole herd surged into motion.

"Jer, watch 'em!" Jake shouted as the longhorns turned first toward the river and then back away from it toward the east. As the wind picked up, battering riders and cattle both with its fury, Jake retreated toward the nearby hills. He hoped to outrace the cattle and join Jericho and Len, but the long-horns were too quick. They poured past him to the east, tearing the night with the din of their hooves. Jake shouted and shouted, but it just wasn't possible to be heard.

In the beginning he wasn't afraid for himself. Clearly Jer and Len were facing the full fury of the stampede. But the wind suddenly shifted. Fresh sheets of rain whipped up out of the south, and to make matters worse, hailstones began whirling through the air.

"Lord, help us!" Jake cried. The spotted mustang whined and bucked as icy pellets peppered its haunches, and Jake fought to stay mounted. To make matters worse, the stam-peding cattle had turned back toward the river. Most were well to the south, but a thousand head cut a wide path, and those on the far flank were rumbling straight toward Jake Wetherby.

"Come on, boy, settle down," Jake pleaded as he pressed his knees hard into the mustang's ribs. The horse reacted by turning. Finally sensing the approaching peril, the horse started to respond. Jake regained control, and he urged the mustang away toward the safety of the nearby hills.

"See there, boy," he cried. "The high ground. The cows'll run to the river and leave us be up there."

The longhorns raced on, throwing up a mixture of mud and dust as the storm gradually saturated the prairie. Jake noticed the noise more than anything. The ground seemed to lurch beneath his horse, and he wondered if he would be able to escape. Steers engulfed him. He could sense the sharp points of horns closing in.

Then, as suddenly as it had begun, the storm seemed to lose its energy. The mustang found its footing and tore toward the hills. At the same time, three riders approached from the hills, waving ropes and turning the longhorns away.

"Thank you, Lord," Jake muttered as he raced past them. He couldn't turn the mustang, even if he'd been inclined to try. The pitiful exhausted animal galloped up the hillside and finally halted, spent, near a clump of scrub oaks.

"Easy, boy," Jake said, stroking the weary animal's neck.

The mustang uttered a low moan and shuddered. Instinctively Jake hopped down. The horse then collapsed.

The moon broke through the clouds overhead, and Jake saw a deep gash in the animal's rump. A second wound opened the poor horse's right side.

"You ran all that way torn half to pieces?" Jake asked, stunned. The horse answered with an agonizing whine. The mustang was bleeding out its life, and Jake didn't even have a rifle to end its suffering.

"Maizy couldn't have done any better by me," Jake declared, stepping closer to the horse. "You saved my life while you were losing yours."

It was as close to showing gratitude as Jake had managed in a long time. He doubted the horse even noticed. It was tormented by waves of pain. Then the animal grew quiet.

"At least your fight's over," Jake said, shuddering. "I got a mile or two yet to go."

10

Jake had barely stripped his saddle from the dead mustang when Jordy and Tip Stuart rode up.

"Thought you dead for sure, Jake," Jordy said, dropping down from his horse and clutching his brother's side. "You were right in the middle of those steers! I—"

"Jer?" Jake interrupted.

"Oh, he's just fine," Jordy said, laughing. "He and Len splashed into the river. Fool longhorns had all the swimming they care for just now."

"Anybody else hurt?" Jake asked.

"Just your horse," Tip said, staring at the animal's corpse. "Fool mustangs. Need a lot more work before they're fit for this trail."

"That horse saved my hide!" Jake barked. "He did just fine."

"With a hair more work, he wouldn't have gotten caught in that pinch," Tip insisted. "Heave your saddle up, Jake. I'll carry it back to camp. You can ride double with Jordy there."

"We've done it before, haven't we, Jake?" Jordy asked, grinning as he remounted his horse.

"A time or two," Jake confessed. "I believe you're growing some, too, little brother."

"Be borrowing a razor off you one of these days."

"Never doubted that," Jake said as he climbed up behind his brother. "You'll be whiskered like an old billy goat any day now."

"Wouldn't go that far," Jordy said, "but I did scratch a chin hair yesterday."

"It's a start," Jake declared. "It's a start."

Jake only half remembered the rest of that night. The whole crew was up past midnight, quieting the stock, and the rain had soaked every stitch of bedding. Even so, Jake had collapsed in the soggy grass near the cook wagon, and he awoke to find himself fully clothed and wrapped in his poncho.

"You're a sight, Jake," little Josh remarked as he roused the cowboys.

"You don't look to've been doing any high living yourself, Peanut," Jake replied.

"At least I kicked off my boots 'fore I went to sleep," Josh said, grinning.

Jake, seeing it was so, had to laugh along.

"I think I've probably got a hailstone or two trapped in my drawers, too," he declared. "Wish I could remember better. Must've been a real exciting night we had!"

Once Jake got to his feet, he realized they were rather late in rising.

"Colonel Duncan and Lofland left at first light," Josh explained. "Put Wash in charge of the outfit."

"Yeah, that explains it," Jake muttered. He knew as well as anyone they should grab a quick breakfast and start rounding up strays. Wash was in no hurry to get started, though.

"There's just five miles or so left to cover," Wash insisted. "The fort's not going anywhere."

"No, but the herd's liable to," Eddie complained. "We had a stampede last night, remember? No tellin' how many ran off into the hills or up and down the river."

"Didn't we have night guards?" Wash asked. "They would have stopped any cattle wandering off."

"Did he hear me?" Eddie asked, turning to the others. "Oh, hellfire and roast chicken! Gene, Jake, let's have ourselves a look while Wash here chews another biscuit."

"Everybody's worn down to a nub," Gene said as he and Jake followed Eddie out to where Tip had picketed the horses. "Don't see how it could hurt to take it slow."

"I'll allow that fool nephew of the colonel to think that way," Eddie grumbled. "You know better, Gene. The sooner we chase in the strays, the closer they'll be. By midmornin' a longhorn can make some distance, and there are hundreds of gullies to hide in between here and Rock Bluff. Lord knows the places up north toward Fort Washita!"

"He's right," Jake reluctantly agreed. "Not much point in the whole outfit going, though."

"No?" Eddie asked.

"For one thing," Tip said, trotting up with Jordy, "we don't have enough good mounts for 'em. Ought to manage three, though."

"Four," Jericho said, joining them.

"Five," Len added.

"You two had a hard night," Gene noted. "Ought to rest some if anybody does."

"You and Jake shared the same watch, didn't you?" Jericho argued. "Anyhow, that Albert fellow got himself started up, and I can't abide wind of that variety."

"He does blow hard sometimes," Gene agreed.

"May have met his match this morning, though," Jericho said, laughing. "Went and got Si started on superstitions. Knowing Si, that Albert's sure to be riding backward and hanging horseshoes on his hat by noon."

They all laughed at the notion. Then Tip picked out mounts and they began saddling the animals. Shortly they were scouring the ravines and hillsides for wandering longhorns.

It was midday before Ty Wells rode out with word that Wash Duncan had finally decided to drive the herd on to Fort Washita. By then Eddie Stuart had supervised the roundup of almost sixty cattle.

"I figure we're still shy twenty of our own beeves," Gene announced, "but we've managed to collect twenty-five mavericks."

"Best get 'em branded before the Chickasaws happen by again," Eddie urged. "I judge they'd figure any stock driven in off their range belong to them."

"Wouldn't you?" Jake asked.

"I confess I would," Eddie agreed. "Get an iron heated, Gene. We'll do it right away."

Jake had to laugh at the hasty way they went about the branding of those range beeves.

"We'd make a fine bunch of cow thieves, wouldn't we?" Gene asked.

"Must be our horse thief ancestry," Tip said. "Comes out in us from time to time."

"We're not really stealing those cows, are we?" Josh asked.

"Nope," Tip explained. "Truth is, they were likely sired by another herd travelin' this trail."

"Must've been a real determined cow got itself a calf on a trail herd," Josh declared. "I thought nobody brings bulls along. Now I don't know everything, being just a cook's boy, but it seems like it'd be a tough business, breedin' with a steer."

Jake grinned, but Ron Callahan dropped to his knees, howling.

"Boy, you got sense," Callahan announced.

While Eddie and Gene got the range cattle branded, Wash ordered the balance of the herd started north. With the colonel gone, Wash returned Martin Albert to left point and took the lead personally.

"Can't lose many cattle off that way this time," Callahan noted as he rode past Jake. "Not with the river there."

"Guess not," Jake replied.

Callahan then eased his way back to where Len Baxter rode covering the right flank. It was reassuring, having a steady man there in Gene's absence, but Jake was nevertheless glad when Gene arrived later to take his usual place riding swing. The herd remained oddly unsettled, and Jake passed most of the afternoon cutting off runaways and chasing them back to the main body. While he was gone, the lead steers had the bad habit of halting.

"Lots of good grass here," Gene said when he rode up to help Jake coax the cows into motion. "And you're not gettin' much help from Albert."

"I gave up expecting miracles," Jake replied. "At least he hasn't run half the herd into the river."

Actually, Albert seemed to be trying, for a change. Jake didn't hold inexperience against the man. After all, half the crew was learning to work cattle as they headed north. His grudge against Albert was that the fellow shirked his duties. He avoided his watch when he could, and he relied on Wash Duncan to excuse his shortcomings. On the other hand, it couldn't be much fun, listening to all the whispered insults and reading the scorn in his companions' eyes.

As Jake rode out to turn a wayward longhorn, he got his first glimpse of Fort Washita. It wasn't the large post Jake had anticipated. Two large stone structures dominated a central parade ground. Smaller log buildings stood opposite, and beyond them a line of rough-hewn cabins and shanties spread out. There was a noticeable lack of soldiers.

Wash would have led the whole outfit straight onto the parade ground. Fortunately Colonel Duncan appeared.

"Turn the herd out here by the river," he told Jake. "Leave them to graze."

"Yes, sir," Jake replied.

Gene rode up, and Jake passed on the colonel's orders. Gene nodded and swung back to tell the others.

The cattle appeared to be as weary as their herders, and for once they responded well to the cowboys' prods and shouts. In half an hour the herd had been neatly formed beside the Washita. There they remained, apparently content to chew buffalo grass and drink at the river.

"Uncle John said we'll rotate the crew," Wash explained as he gathered the outfit. "He wants you, Tip, to meet him at the trader's corral and look over some horses. Doc, I need a list of any supplies you need. Eddie, choose which men you want to ride guard. The rest of you give your horses a rest."

"We'll all do that," Eddie added. "We'll make camp on that rise above the fort. For a time, the cows will stay calm enough. In an hour or so we'll mount four men and ride the flanks, just like yesterday."

"Uncle John—" Wash objected.

"You want to do this?" Eddie asked angrily. "Thought not. Get along to the traders with you, Wash, and leave me to look after the cattle."

"Got to eyeball some ponies," Tip said, grinning at his brother.

"I expect we'll pass a couple of days here," Eddie said when Wash turned and started toward the fort. "I hear there's good fishin' in the river and tolerable turkey shootin' beyond. I expect somethin' better to eat than dried beef."

"You complainin' about my cookin'?" Doc barked.

"Nope," Eddie insisted. "Just the variety of your table."

The men followed Doc Trimble's wagon to the nearby hill. There they hurriedly made camp and noted their guard shifts. Jake found himself and his brothers free those next three hours, and he eagerly led them down to the river to wash away the sweat and grime.

"Wouldn't hurt to give our clothes a scrub, either," Josh declared as he held out a cake of lye soap. "Borrowed her off Doc. He says there are ladies at the fort. Got to look our best, don't you think?"

Jake nodded his agreement. After scrubbing flesh and cloth, they hung up their clothes in the branches of nearby oaks and willows. Jake then produced several hooked lines, and the Wetherbys passed the remainder of their free time snagging catfish from the Washita.

Jake didn't get a look at the fort itself until that next day. He'd passed the evening helping Doc fry catfish so Josh could accompany Jordy and Tip on a horse-buying expedition to a nearby Chickasaw ranch. They returned with seven fine animals, each purchased at a lamentably high price.

"They're better than those nags the trader offered you, Colonel," Tip insisted when John Duncan complained of the price.

"Seems to me everything in the Nations is high on cost and low on performance," Wash grumbled as he took a pull at a jug of Washita corn liquor.

"That'll be the last spirits anybody buys short of trail's

end,'' Colonel Duncan declared. "Makes for bad feelings, and it dulls a man's senses. He needs to stay sharp as we get on up the trail.''

"Colonel, we're still thin on horses,'' Tip observed, frowning. "We'll end up overworkin' these new ones if we don't add a few more.''

"How many?'' the colonel asked.

"Five might do,'' Tip answered. "Seven'd be better.''

"Won't the day's rest be enough?'' Wash asked.

"It's sure to help heal the saddle sores, but it won't mend tendons,'' Tip explained.

"We'll leave the worst of the animals here,'' John Duncan said, sighing. "Won't cost much to board them, and we'll pick them up on the way back south.''

It seemed a good notion, but Jake was heartbroken when he found Maizy was among the animals Tip deemed unfit for the trail north.

"She's a good horse,'' Jake argued. "Has carried me through many a storm.''

"She will again, too, if you give her a rest,'' Jordy noted. "Now, let's have a look at the fort. I hear it's full of Indians. They've got rock candy at the trading post. I could do with a taste of sugar just now.''

Jordy had a second motive, too, though. The trader had a roan stallion with a splash of white across his forehead.

"It's a beautiful horse, isn't it?'' Jordy asked as he clambered up a fence rail and gazed fondly at the stallion.

"I don't think there's enough money left in the colonel's pocket to buy him, though,'' Jake observed. "That's breeding stock there.''

"No, that animal's a curse,'' a large, heavyset man with a full beard declared.

"You the trader?'' Jordy asked.

"Lewis Parrott,'' the man announced. "Trader and fool of a horse buyer.''

"I'm Jake Wetherby,'' Jake explained. "This is my brother Jordan.''

"I hear you've got a standing bet concerning that stallion," Jordy said, hopping down and gazing up into the trader's eyes.

"Sure do," Parrott replied. "Anybody who can stay atop that demon five minutes is welcome to ride away on him."

"What's the catch?" Jake asked.

"I don't pay for broken bones," Parrott answered, laughing. "And I charge folks two bits to watch."

"I aim to have a try at him," Jordy declared.

"Now, I don't know about that," Parrott said, growing concerned. "You see him real peaceful, son, but he's a genuine outlaw. He'll throw you ten feet and stomp you for good measure. I couldn't let a boy at him. Not in good conscience."

"I can ride him," Jordy boasted. "I feel it."

"Others a lot older've thought that," Parrott insisted.

"If my brother says he can do it, he can," Jake told the trader. "He's half horse himself."

"He's your brother," Parrott muttered. "If you deem him up to the challenge, who am I to turn good money away?"

Parrott then told them to return in two hours' time. By then he'd spread the word. Most of the soldiers were off chasing a band of prowling Comanches, but the dozen or so remaining climbed the corral rails as did twenty-five Chickasaw visitors and most of the traders.

"Jordy, you ought to reconsider," Jake urged as he eyed the stallion. Something had stirred the animal up, and it was stomping around, snorting and clawing at the dusty ground.

"I can ride him," Jordy said, pulling out a rope as he slipped between the rails and approached the stallion.

"Fool youngster," a weathered old sergeant said. "Most likely he'll never even get mounted."

Jordy approached the horse dead on, whispering the whole time. He took each step slowly, with considerable caution.

"What is it, fellow?" he called. "What's got you so anxious? Can't be a half-grown little fellow like me!"

His calm voice seemed to relax the horse, and Jordy slipped his rope over the animal's head easily enough. He then brushed the roan's neck and moved along to the right foreleg.

"Here's the problem, eh?" Jordy said, lifting the leg. He pried an embedded stone from the hoof and tossed it away.

"Trader's got more tricks'n that, sonny!" a private hollered.

Jordy took a deep breath and climbed the big stallion's back. For just an instant the horse seemed willing to accept its new burden. Then, quick as lightning, it began bucking.

"Easy, boy," Jordy called as he hung on for dear life. "Easy! I'm nobody to hurt you!"

"Won't be much longer now!" the sergeant declared.

Men were wagering right and left. Jake was too broke and far too nervous to join in. Tip Stuart bet fifteen dollars on Jordy, though, receiving four-to-one odds.

"Anybody watchin' the time?" Tip howled.

"Am now," the sergeant said.

The roan raced around the corral, bucking and shaking, trying every maneuver it could think of to dislodge its small rider. Jordy hung on tenaciously.

"He's like a seed tick on a hound!" the sergeant cried. "I believe he'll last."

He did, too. When the sergeant announced five minutes had passed, the crowd grumbled.

"You can get off now, son," Parrott called.

"I aim to ride this horse!" Jordy shouted. And he dug in his heels and outlasted the stallion. In the end the roan calmed down, and Jordy managed to nudge him into a gentle canter.

"I'll be!" the sergeant cried, adding a well-chosen curse or two as well.

"I'll call him Buster," Jordy announced.

"He didn't bust you, little brother," Jake declared proudly.

"No, he's made us rich," Tip said, waving a handful of bank notes in the air.

"Told you I'd ride him," Jordy told Jake.

"You sure did," Jake replied. "Guess I'd better hone up that razor for you. Buy you some new clothes. You've gone and stretched yourself taller."

11

The brief layover at Fort Washita provided more than fresh mounts. The cattle had themselves a good feed, and the crew caught some extra sleep. When they started the herd north that next morning, Jake felt revived. He noticed even Martin Albert seemed eager to renew the drive, and Jordy climbed atop Buster with a genuine glimmer of enthusiasm.

Jake himself found it odd, saddling the bay gelding Colonel Duncan had assigned him.

"Jacob Henry, you'd do better not to name this one," the colonel advised. "The trail ahead's steep, and we may be trading out horses again before we're finished."

Jake nodded his agreement, and he tried to get by calling the animal "Horse." It didn't work, though. By and by he grew attached to the gelding in spite of himself, and Jordy didn't help by dubbing the bay "Bailey."

"Why call it that?" Jake asked.

"He's a bay, isn't he?" Jordy asked. "Couldn't come by anything better."

So, riding right point, Jake made his way north and east atop Bailey. He steered the herd across the low flats beyond the Washita River and on north toward Clear Creek. They made better than ten miles each of those next three days, arriving at the creek on schedule.

Jake was busy grouping the cattle in a sea of white and yellow wildflowers alongside the stream when Charlie Berry appeared with a handful of riders. Only one had been with him the last time, and Jake guessed correctly these were the Choctaws.

"These must be even more civilized than the last batch," Jordy observed an hour later when he and Jake dragged their blanket rolls out of the cook wagon. "Dressed in homespun and wearing leather boots. You can hardly tell they're Indians."

"Truth is, they're better'n most o' the whites you find up in the Nations," Doc Trimble grumbled. "Horse thieves and road agents! Don't feel obliged to mind the tribal police, and the lawmen from Arkansas and Texas have no authority here."

"That's not comforting news," Jake remarked.

"Don't trouble yourself any about it, son," Stan Lofland said as he accepted a cold biscuit from Josh. "That's why the colonel brought his own law along."

Jake winced. He recalled all too painfully the cattle thieves hung a year before on the Trinity. They might have earned their end, but one had been very young, and Jake deemed the colonel had been unnaturally harsh.

"We can't just let them go," Duncan had insisted. "They'll only hit the next bunch to come through here. Cattlemen have the obligation to clear the range of bandits."

Jake swept the memory from his brain as he sat across from the cook fire with Jericho, Si, and Jordy. Those other cowboys not assigned to late afternoon watch joined them. Before Jer could strike up a tune on his guitar, Wash Duncan stumbled over, muttering a curse under his breath.

"We're entertaining guests," Wash announced, nodding toward the creek. Colonel Duncan stood chatting with a handful of Choctaws there. "Uncle John says set an extra kettle on the fire."

"Anything wrong?" Lofland growled.

"Seems like we have to pay this batch, too," Wash complained. "Fifty more dollars to that Berry fellow, and these fellows want a hundred themselves."

"It's their land, remember?" Eddie whispered. "Seems a fair enough price, too, since we're crossin' a lot more Choctaw territory and our beeves are eatin' more o' their grass."

"I'll be glad to get back to Texas," Wash declared. "No one holds you up on the way to market there."

"I don't know any farmers who'd welcome you onto their fields, though," Jericho whispered. "You, Jake?"

"Oh, but Wash there's such a pleasant fellow to dicker with," Jake replied.

"I don't know about the rest of you," Gene said, joining them, "but *I* sure do wish Wash was back in Texas. He could take that sidekick Albert along with him, too."

They shared a laugh.

As it turned out, the Choctaws were good company.

"What's for dinner, Doc?" Colonel Duncan asked when he led the Indians to the fire.

"Beef, beans, and biscuits," Doc answered. "Unless one of these boys shot us a turkey today."

"Turkey?" the leader of the Choctaws, a youngish fellow with a trace of red to his hair, asked. "We can do better than that."

Before Doc could bark a reply, a pair of Choctaw boys climbed up the steep bank of Clear Creek dragging a deer carcass between them. Smaller youngsters followed with baskets of river catfish and small perch. Three women completed the party.

Jake watched speechless as the women took charge of the cooking. Doc, flabbergasted, retreated to his wagon and looked on helplessly as the Indian boys dug a shallow pit. Their mothers then buried the fish under a layer of coals. Next they began butchering the deer carcass.

"Venison steaks," Gene said, licking his lips.

"This is the sort of company I like," Jake declared. "They'd be welcome at my camp anytime."

Once they'd eaten, the real entertainment commenced. The Choctaw leader, who called himself Jefferson Rivers, laid out a race course on the north side of the creek, and the younger Choctaws raced ponies. Others rode along, shouting wildly and offering an occasional taunt as they performed unbelievable stunts on horseback.

"My son Donald offers a challenge," Rivers told the cowboys. "He's got a fast horse, and he'd race anybody who cares to test himself."

"That's me," Jordy boasted, springing to his feet.

"Hold up a minute, boy," Colonel Duncan cautioned. "You have to understand a couple of things. First of all, up here if you race, you wager your mount. Second, a Choctaw race has a way of getting out of hand. There aren't many rules. Just winning. Truth is, it's more combat than speed."

"Yeah, I noticed that," Jordy said, nodding. "I've been watching them. The trick's to get out early and stay in front. Those are good horses yonder. I guess you might buy 'em off me if I won."

"Guess I should've warned you, Colonel," Jake said, grinning. "Jordy's got an itch to be rich."

"Glad to see it," Colonel Duncan declared. "Most cowboys have a powerful shortage of ambition. You win the ponies, Josh, and I'll buy them. And if you lose, well, you aren't any worse off than if you hadn't stayed atop the horse back at the fort."

Others might have agreed. Not Jake. He knew Jordy had taken Buster to heart. That was no small thing, not for a Wetherby. And especially not for the younger ones. Josh and Jordy had both lost too many people in their young lives to latch onto anybody very easily. It hurt too much losing them. Easier to shy away.

"You understand, Jordy?" Jake asked.

"Don't plan to lose," Jordy boasted. "Buster won't let me."

"That horse had a hard day's ride, little brother. Might be better to give him the evening to rest up."

"Ten miles is nothing to Buster," Jordy boasted as he turned to leave.

Jake frowned. There were no certainties when you took on something new.

Jordy had fewer doubts, though. He dashed off to the remuda. When he returned, leading Buster, the young Choctaws looked over with interest.

"It's going to be a horse race," Rivers declared. "Donald?"

"A good horse," the Choctaw boy observed. "Mine, too," he added, pointing out a spotted stallion grazing on the far bank of the creek.

"Let's walk the course," Rivers suggested.

Jordy followed Donald. Three other Choctaw boys hurried along behind.

It was a challenging route, full of sharp turns and rough terrain. At certain points Choctaws stood watch. Jake assigned a brother or a friend to each.

"Just to make sure," Jake explained to Rivers.

"Never smart to take chances," Rivers observed. "Especially when there are good horses at stake."

There was little else Jake could do to help, though. The rest was up to Jordy. As he mounted his half-wild stallion, the boy seemed too small for the task. The Choctaw riders were taller, with a hard edge to their jaws. Their muscular shoulders and sinewy forearms seemed better prepared for the task at hand.

"Don't worry," Josh whispered as he hopped over beside Jake. "You wouldn't have thought he could stay on top of Buster back at the fort, but he did. Jordy's not any too tall, but he knows horses. I wouldn't bet against him."

"He does look determined, doesn't he?" Jake noted.

"Generally gets a thing done when he sets out at it like that," Joseph added. "It's a Wetherby trait."

Jake thought of their father's countless grand schemes. They had all ended in failure.

We'll be different, Jake had vowed. He supposed Jordy aimed to prove it.

Rivers formed the young riders in a single line and raised a white cloth. When he dropped the cloth, the riders set off with a howl. Almost immediately two of the slower ones tried to retard Jordy's progress, but the yellow-haired youngster sniffed out the trick, turned Buster sharply, and eluded both. Buster then made a quick sprint past a third horse and pulled even with young Rivers.

"Go, Jordy!" Josh shouted. "Show 'em!"

There was a sharp bend just ahead, and Jordy disappeared behind a stand of cottonwoods.

"All we can do now is wait for 'em to start back," Jake muttered.

"Don't worry," Josh said, laughing. "They left those other three behind. It's just Jordy and the chief's boy now."

"Seems to me that's plenty to worry about," Jake replied. "Wish I could be as sure as you are, Peanut."

"Won't do any good, worrying," Josh insisted. "Better to yell and jump around. Anyhow, it's not like he went and bet you or me. It's only a horse."

Jake tried to laugh, but he managed only a nervous gurgle. He paced back and forth along the creek bank as he waited for Josh to reappear. He felt his breathing grow shallow, and he clawed at his side with nervous fingers.

"There he is!" Josh shouted as Buster emerged from a low rise and hurried along toward the creek. Donald Rivers was close behind, and Jake noticed a lash in the young Choctaw's hand. Red streaks marked Jordy's face, and his shirt was torn above and below his left shoulder.

"Jake?" Josh asked, noticing.

"Yeah," Jake said, scowling. "I worried about such tricks."

But Jordy eluded young Rivers's next stroke, and Buster pulled farther away. There was a boulder in the path a hundred yards ahead, and Josh skillfully waited until the final moment before turning to avoid the rock. Donald Rivers had less warning, for Buster threw up a storm of dust in his wake. The Choctaw rider had to haul back hard on his pony's reins, and the horse reared up and bucked. Donald Rivers tried to discard his whip and grab the reins with both hands, but it was too late. He went flying up and over his mount's rump.

There was a hush among the Choctaws as they strained to detect horse and rider amid the swirling dust. Finally they sighed with relief as Donald stumbled out into view, calling helplessly after his horse. The Choctaw pony had fled toward the creek, leaving its rider behind.

Jordy galloped on along and easily swept past the finish line, winning the race. The other Choctaw riders trotted in a few minutes later.

"Ayyyy!" the Choctaws howled as they glimpsed Jordy at the creek, stroking Buster's nose.

"He's a rider, all right!" Eddie Stuart yelled as he splashed across the creek. Jake wasn't far behind. When he reached his brother's side, Jake helped Jordy down and gazed hard at three welts striping his back.

"You warned me," Jordy said, wincing as Jake touched the tender flesh.

"You won anyway, though," Jake observed. "I'm proud of you."

"Can I trust you to dicker with Colonel Duncan over the ponies, then?" Jake asked. "I think I'd like to see Doc about my shoulder."

"Sure," Jake said, turning Jordy over to Josh.

"I'll tend Buster," Jericho volunteered.

"Here," Jordy said, pulling a cube of sugar from his pocket. "See he gets this. I promised him a sweet lick."

"I'd say he earned it," Jer declared.

As they scattered, each to his individual task, Jake glanced back at the Choctaws. Donald Rivers hung his head and sheepishly approached his father. The older Rivers then stepped toward Jake.

"Your brother?" the older Rivers asked. "Where would he have us bring his ponies?"

"I'll take 'em," Jake replied. "He's gone to get . . . some doctoring."

Jake tried to fight the anger from his eyes. He wasn't altogether successful.

"My son values his stallion," Rivers went on. "He's lost fairly, but he asks you consider allowing him to buy back the animal."

"I raised him," Donald explained. "From his birthing. He and I, uh, are more than horse and rider."

"Jordy would understand that," Jake noted. "He and Buster are the same."

"That's clear to everyone," Rivers observed. "Have you a price in mind?"

"I'm no horse buyer," Jake replied. "And not much good at dickering."

"Well, I've bought a few horses and sold many others," Rivers said, "and I guess even in Indian Territory, that stallion's worth fifty dollars. More even. Would your brother accept sixty?"

"I'd say that's more than fair, sir," Jake answered. "Make it the fifty. I guess Jordy'd likely make the horse a present to you if it wouldn't hurt your feelings."

"We'd have to return such generosity," Rivers explained.

"Well, times being what they are, it's best I take the money," Jake declared.

"It's a bargain well made," Rivers said, offering his hand.

Jake shook the Choctaw's hand and nodded to young Donald. Jake then took charge of the other three animals and led them across to the south bank of Clear Creek. John Duncan offered fifteen dollars for each, and Jake turned the ninety-five dollars over to Jordy later that night.

"We've turned to the wrong trade, Jake," Gene declared afterward. "We ought to've taken up horse racin'."

"Speak for yourself," Jake answered. "Horses and I have an understanding. They leave me to stay atop 'em so long as I don't ask too much."

"I noticed that," Gene observed. "Maybe Jordy could teach you a thing or two about 'em."

"No, I consider myself well past learning," Jake insisted. "Now let's find ourselves some rest. The colonel's sure to have us on the trail early tomorrow."

"That's a bet you'd win every time," Gene muttered. "Every single time."

12

That next day John Duncan did start his cattle north early. They had worked their way back to what some called the Texas Road now, and the going was easier. The longhorns were finally broken to the trail. They plodded along slowly, but there were fewer strays to chase in. Moreover, the animals barely noticed passing riders, freight wagons, or passenger coaches.

"Be in Boggy Depot by late afternoon," Gene whispered when he joined Jake for a time around midday.

"What's that?" Jake asked.

"Stage station," Gene explained. "Freight stop. They've got a federal post office there, too. A real lively spot, to hear folks talk."

"Lively?" Jake asked. "How so?"

"They've got almost every sort of entertainment a cowboy could ask after, Jake. Loads of saloons. Gamblin'."

"I don't have any money to spare for gambling," Jake replied. "And spirits don't much agree with me."

"They also got a bawdy house," Gene added. "Miss Flora's Palace of Elegant Amusement."

"What?"

"I hear they've got lace curtains and silver teapots in the place. Also got girls, of course."

"You mean ones you pay for?"

"Well, you mostly pay for 'em, one way or another, Jake. You ever been around one for long you didn't wind up spendin' money on?"

"I never spent any money on Miranda," Jake insisted.

"I bet you never even got her to kiss you!" Gene cried. "These gals'll be downright friendly."

"I don't know about this, Gene. Doesn't feel right, and besides, I'm broke."

"Shoot, Jake, I'll loan you a dollar myself. May be the last time we see a halfway decent woman for weeks."

"I'll think on it," Jake promised.

"Don't think too long," Gene warned. "We won't be here forever."

By the time they moved the herd the ten or so miles to Muddy Boggy Creek, the whole outfit was gabbing away about Miss Flora's.

"Best set aside your talk and get the herd settled in!" Colonel Duncan growled.

"Weren't you ever young, Colonel?" Eddie asked.

"Never as young as some of these boys," the colonel answered. "I'm not foolish enough to hurry you into drowning water, either. It would be best to keep to camp when you're not on watch."

Colonel Duncan did more than issue advice. He doubled the guard, claiming Boggy Depot was a rustler's haven, and he refused to advance anybody so much as a penny against their wages.

"Ah, Colonel, we've not seen anything but steer rumps and Indians since leavin' Texas," Ron Callahan complained. "Don't seem so much to give us a dollar or two."

"I did that once, and I ended up with half an outfit stumble-footed drunk!"

Nevertheless, Wash Duncan and Martin Albert rode into the depot before the herd was even secured, and the colonel wasn't long in following them.

"Never says a word to that nephew o' his," Eddie complained. "Well, I've got first watch, so I'll be busy for a time. I swear I'm goin' in afterward, though."

"Be near midnight," Callahan grumbled.

"You figure Miss Flora closes early?" Eddie asked. "No, she'll just be gettin' started up 'round then."

Jake and his brothers were assigned the late watch, probably because Duncan thought them less likely to stray under their brother's watchful eye. If so, the colonel either overestimated Jake's hold or forgot Jordy had ninety-five hot dollars burning in his pocket.

"You boys just bound and determined to get yourselves into trouble, aren't you?" Stan Lofland observed when the Weatherbys and Si Garrett prepared to walk into Boggy Depot.

"Did the Colonel tell you to stop us?" Jake asked.

"You figure that's possible, Jake?" Lofland asked, grinning.

"Might be," Jake said, eyeing the gunman's pistols.

"I don't get paid to shoot youngsters," Lofland said, laughing. "Truth is, I thought I might go along."

"You'd be mighty welcome," Si said. "Not that we don't know our way around, but we'd be glad to have a man along who's been up the trail before."

"I see," Lofland said, fighting to chase a smile from his lips. "Well, one thing you might take into account is that women aren't particular fond of men that smell of cow dung. Best to head downstream and wash first. Put on those new duds you bought at Fort Washita. Make a good impression. That's the thing."

"Sounds wise," Jordy readily agreed. "Anything else?"

"Stay together," Lofland advised. "It's real easy in a trail town for a lone man to get himself clubbed and robbed. Why, I recollect a fellow we found stripped bare one morning down in San Antonio. Got himself a little drunk, and thieves took everything he owned."

"This doesn't sound like too friendly a place," Jake noted.

"Oh, they're eager enough to take your money, but it's best to be careful. A man can get himself killed real easy. Little law and plenty of trouble."

"Maybe we should stay in camp," Jake said, eyeing his brothers.

"I'm sure going," Si insisted.

"Me, too," Jericho piped in.

"Jake, we came up here to find some adventure," Jordy added. "Don't this sound like it to you? Does to me."

"Next thing you'll tell me Josh ought to come, too," Jake complained.

"No, he's got too much work to get done," Jordy explained. "I gave him most of my money to watch."

"That was smart," Lofland declared. "Another thing. Don't tote any guns with you. You're safer without 'em."

"But if there's trouble—" Jericho argued.

"You'd just get shot, son," Lofland barked. "You got anything worth dying for on you? No. Let's head up the creek and get washed now. If we don't start for the depot 'fore long, we'll be due back at the herd before we get anywhere."

And so the Wetherbys scrubbed trail dust and dung smell from their hides and donned themselves in their best clothes. Time was spared to polish boots and brush hats. When Jake, Jer, and Jordy headed into Boggy Depot with Si and Stan Lofland, they appeared more like a family of St. Louis bankers than a band of dusty cowboys up the trail from Texas.

All in all, Boggy Depot proved a disappointment. There were a few log cabins, the freight and stage depot, and a small church. A hair farther along someone had thrown together a clapboard saloon. As for Miss Flora's, it proved to be a canvas tent stretched over pine floorboards.

"Lace curtains?" Jake cried. "Silver teapots?"

"Looks like that's not the only thing got exaggerated," Jer said, pointing to a rather round-faced woman smoking a cigar in the open flap that served as a door.

"Miz Flora?" Si called.

"What can I do for you boys?" she asked, taking a deep breath and puffing up her considerable chest.

"Could we have a look at the gals?" Si asked, stumbling toward the tent with wide eyes.

"Carrie!" Flora called. "Agnes?"

Two rather snaggle-toothed women in their late twenties emerged from the tent, and Si froze.

"Lordy," Jer said, backing away.

"Come along now, boys," Flora urged. "I believe we can

satisfy your needs. You brothers? We might even extend you a family price."

"This isn't what I figured," Jordy said, making a quick dash toward the saloon.

"A bit worse for wear, aren't they?" Lofland asked. "Well, it figures. That Albert got here early and talked 'em old."

Jake managed to grin.

"Jake?" Jericho called.

"I believe I'd better look out for Jordy," Jake replied.

"Me, too," Jericho said, heading for the saloon.

"Sorry, ma'am," Si said, tipping his hat. "They're the only ones with any money."

"And you, sir?" Flora called toward Lofland.

"I never knew the desperation to pay for company," Lofland explained with a grin. "We've got a second watch coming in, though. That batch has a little more seasoning, so the night may not be a total loss."

"Sure," Flora said, taking another puff on her cigar.

"I guess we're not as old as we sometimes think," Jake said as he followed Lofland inside the saloon.

"There are things that oughtn't to be hurried," Lofland noted. "Colonel Duncan says Miss Miranda's developed some strong feelings toward you. A man could do a far sight worse than become John Duncan's son-in-law. Look how he favors Wash, and that fool's not got a notion of how to run cattle. Or much else."

"I might scribble Miranda a note," Jake said, sighing. "They could send it south at the post office."

"I bet they could," Lofland agreed.

Jake bought himself a lemonade and gravitated to the back of the saloon.

"Evening, Colonel," Jake said when he noticed the Duncans sitting at the next table. "You wouldn't know where I could come by some writing paper, would you?"

"As it happens, I do," Duncan answered. "Just asked after it myself. I thought to send Miranda a note."

"Me, too," Jake explained.

"I believe she'd appreciate that," the colonel said, smiling. "There's a clerk's table yonder past the piano player. He'll loan you his pen and some paper. Just give him this."

Colonel Duncan handed Jake two bits. Jake smiled his thanks and headed for the clerk's table. A bewhiskered man with a balding head and thick spectacles turned his desk over to Jake.

"Thanks, sir," Jake said, handing over the quarter.

"You're welcome to it, son," the clerk told Jake. "Doesn't get much use around her. Not one man in five can write."

Jake glanced at the nearby tables and studied the men. There was a gray mist of cigar and cigarette smoke shrouding them, but Jake noted most of the men appeared unshaven, unwashed, and unfriendly. Their dark eyes were oddly evasive, and most carried pistols or knives in their belts.

Si and Jericho had wandered back to the table Jake had just left. Lofland was sitting at the bar, sipping a small glass of yellowish-looking spirits. Jordy was at his side, studying the card players at a nearby table.

Jake stepped over and tapped Jordy on the arm.

"Maybe you best come back here with me," Jake suggested.

"He'll be all right here," Lofland said, interceding. "You get your letter written. Let me be big brother for a while."

Jake grinned his gratitude and returned to the clerk's desk. As he penned the letter, he found himself recalling Miranda's many kindnesses. Most of the letter told of his brothers, though. He wrote about the horse race at Clear Creek and how Jordy outlasted Buster at Fort Washita. He told her the colonel was faring well. Toward the end, Jake added a few lines about himself.

"I'm pulling my weight and learning the cattle trade," he noted. "So far I'm well and safe. I miss you, Miranda, and look forward to seeing you when we return to Texas."

In school he'd been taught to close a letter, "Your obedient servant." That seemed much too formal. He simply scribbled, "Your friend and admirer, Jacob Henry Wetherby."

Just as he completed the final curve of the y, a commotion drew his attention.

"He's givin' my cards away!" a big man dressed in buckskins stormed, drawing a knife and taking a swipe at Jordy.

"Jake!" the boy cried as he leaped out of the way.

Jake made a rush toward the card table, but a rough-looking man dressed in farmer's overalls threw out a leg and tripped him. Jake gazed across the floor at his little brother. Jordy lay sprawled on the floor, and the buckskin-clad giant knelt down and pressed the knife against the youngster's chest.

"I didn't mean anything," Jordy babbled. "I was only watching. I swear. I wasn't saying or doing anything."

"I don't like children," the cardplayer howled. "Boys oughtn't to be in here! Maybe I'll just carve on you some so you'll remember to stay out of the way!"

The big man raised his knife. A single shot exploded through the room. The big man yelped in pain as the knife tumbled from his bloody hand. Two fingers were gone—neatly sliced off by a single bullet.

"That's about enough!" Lofland shouted, helping Jordy to his feet. "Boy told you he was only watching. Haven't you got ears, mister?"

"What I've got is friends," the wounded cardplayer grunted.

"Anybody else taking a hand in this?" Lofland asked, studying the faces of the other men. Colonel Duncan slowly rose from his table, pistol in hand.

"Mr. Lofland here's got friends, too," the colonel explained.

"Lofland?" one of the other cardplayers gasped. "Stan Lofland?"

"That's my name," Lofland confessed. "I know you?"

"No, sir," the gambler replied.

"I won't have these boys bothered," Lofland insisted.

"Why, I agree with you, Mr. Lofland," the gambler said, shuddering. "Maybe I can buy you a drink. Whiskey, the good stuff," he told the bartender. "Help to steady your nerves."

"What about me, Polk?" the wounded man cried.

"Seems to me, considering the possibilities, you came off right light," the man called Polk replied. "Get on out of here before you bloody the floor. Have Flora stitch you up. She's good at that."

The maimed giant staggered out of the saloon, and things settled down.

"I believe it's time we were leaving ourselves," Lofland announced as he downed the whiskey. "Jake, figure you can lasso your brothers?"

"Sure," Jake said, returning to the desk long enough to grab his letter. He then collected Jordy and Jer. Si trotted along behind. Lofland brought up the rear, holding a pistol in his right hand the entire time.

"A wise man takes precautions," Lofland explained once they cleared the town.

"Thanks, Mr. Lofland," Jordy said, gratefully offering his hand.

"Seemed to me a pure waste losing a boy with your talent for winning horse races," Lofland observed as he shook Jordy's hand. "I'd never take it into my head to warn you away from a thing, boys, but I trust tonight you learned for yourselves. Stay away from such places. Too many ways a man can get killed when he mixes cards and whiskey. And women. They're no fit places for youngsters."

"I'm eighteen," Si declared.

"I'm close to that old myself," Jericho added.

"You've both gotten more years than little Ollie," Jake noted. "Mr. Lofland here's right. We're not used to saloons, and we'd do better to avoid them."

"Maybe," Si admitted. "Still, you can't put off everything. If you're going to be a man, you're expected to—"

"What?" Lofland asked. "Get killed? I shot my first man when I was just sixteen. Sixteen, for God's sake. How many since, I don't even know. Is that what you're hurrying yourselves toward? Don't. It's no road you'll enjoy."

Jake gazed into Stan Lofland's tormented eyes and saw pain. Fear, too. He never expected to find either.

"Coming, Jake?" Jordy called as the others continued toward the camp.

"Sure," Jake said, trotting after them.

Stan Lofland hung back, watching the town. Studying shadows.

13

After riding the midnight watch, Jake dove into his blankets, exhausted. In spite of his fatigue, he passed a fitful night. Twice he awoke when Jordy cried out.

"You just had yourself another bad dream," Jake assured his trembling brother.

"It was that gambler with the knife," Jordy said, shuddering. "I could feel the blade in my chest this time."

"Doesn't look to me like you're bleeding any," Jake observed. "That fellow isn't going to bother anybody now. Lofland saw to that."

"Sure," Jordy muttered. "I know that, Jake. Just don't seem to be able to convince my dream of it."

Jake grinned. "Let's take a walk down to the creek, Jordy. Work the scare off you."

"Huh?"

"We'll wear ourselves down so we're too tired for any nightmares," Jake explained.

"I never heard of that," Jordy complained as he pushed aside his blankets.

"It's worked for me plenty of times," Jake insisted.

"You don't have nightmares, Jake. You don't get scared."

"Sure I do. I just hide it better. Now, come along and try it."

"Don't suppose there's anything to lose," Jordy said, shrugging his shoulders.

"Sure there's not. To tell the truth, Jordy, I can't believe anybody who could sit atop a wild stallion or race a batch of Choctaw riders would be scared of any white man."

"He was pretty big, Jake."

"Yeah, he was," Jake admitted. "Maybe we better walk a hair more than usual."

The walk did seem to settle Jordy, and he slept well enough when they returned. It left Jake downright weary when morning came, though.

"Got a herd waiting, Jacob Henry," Colonel Duncan said when he shook Jake to life during breakfast. "Think you can stay awake long enough to get mounted?"

"Any choice?" Jake asked.

"No," the colonel told him.

"Then I guess I best get to it," Jake said, shaking himself alert. "Colonel, I got a letter written to Miranda. You suppose I can stop off at the post office and send it south?"

"We'll do even better," Duncan declared. "I've got one of my own to send. I'll hand both to R. C. Smith. He's driving freight to Dallas, and he'll see the letters are properly delivered."

"Thanks, sir."

"Meanwhile, find that bay and get atop it," the colonel ordered. "We've got a creek to cross and miles to cover."

They passed those next three days winding their way through the hills west of the Jack Fork Mountains. The grass there was rich, and John Duncan insisted on grazing the cattle every hour or so. Even so, the crew was accustomed to its work now, and they had little difficulty urging the cattle up the trail. They reached McAlester's store south of the Canadian River the second week of June.

"You've done well, boys," Colonel Duncan declared as they bedded down the herd. "Country ahead flattens out, and we'll make fine time."

"Got rivers to cross, though," Callahan noted. "The Canadian and the Arkansas can both run deep this early in the summer."

"They can," Colonel Duncan admitted. "But we're used to crossing streams now, and so are the cattle. We'll manage it all right."

Jake shared the colonel's optimism. The miles seemed to

be flying by beneath their feet now. Horses and men were wearing down some, but the cattle were fattening up nicely. St. Louis was still a long way away, he realized, but just then he suspected they would do fine even if they had to drive that herd all the way to Chicago.

Once camp was made, Colonel Duncan and Stan Lofland escorted Doc Trimble's wagon on to McAlester's. Josh remained behind to build a cook fire and start dinner.

"You think the colonel's expecting trouble?" Josh asked Jake when the wagon rolled out of view.

"Don't think so," Jake replied.

"I wouldn't bet against it," Si said, joining them. "Took Lofland along, didn't he?"

"Left the rifles behind, too," Josh pointed out.

Jake noted both arguments and set off to locate Eddie.

"I'd say you're right," Eddie said when Jake shared his news. "I saw a couple of fellows skirtin' the herd a while back. Just thought 'em wayfarers, but now that you mention it, they didn't seem the travelin' types."

"I'll ride out and alert the riders," Jake said.

"Talk to Wash first," Eddie urged. "He's in charge."

"And where is he?"

"I figured he and Albert went in with the colonel, but now I'm not so sure. Who's got the guns?"

"They're in camp," Jake explained. "With the chuck box."

"Let's have a look after Wash, Jake," Eddie suggested. "If we can't find him, let's arm the men and put together a plan. I don't favor lettin' 'em come in and scatter our herd."

"Me, neither," Jake grumbled. "We've brought 'em too far to lose out now."

They located Wash Duncan sipping coffee at the cook fire.

"I haven't seen anybody," Wash declared. "Why panic? Uncle John's close by. Leave him to worry about raiders."

"I wouldn't care to ride guard unarmed with rustlers about," Eddie argued. "It's only smart to pair the men up."

"I can take the rifles out to them," Jake volunteered. "Wouldn't take me a quarter hour."

"You have to let 'em know what they're up against," Eddie insisted.

"Well, it's no skin off my nose," Wash replied. "But warn 'em about starting a stampede. No shooting if they can help it."

"I'll do that," Jake vowed. "None of our outfit will fire first. But if somebody else starts it up—"

"They're free to defend themselves, of course," Wash agreed. "The harm will already be done."

Eddie and Si helped tie six rifles behind Jake's saddle.

"Remember," Eddie warned. "Pair up the riders. Tell 'em to watch the western horizon carefully. The sun's startin' to set, and it'll mask a man's movements off that way."

"I know what to do," Jake assured his companions. "Eddie, you be sure and organize the others. The few of us out with the herd won't put raiders off for long."

"We'll be along," Eddie promised. "Now hurry. And if it comes to a fight, trust Gene to handle things. He's been in tight spots before."

I've been in one or two myself, Jake thought as he mounted Bailey. With Lofland and the colonel gone, though, the herd was particularly vulnerable.

Jake made his way around the rim of the herd with great caution. He met Jericho on the south edge and waved him alongside.

"What's wrong?" Jer asked when he edged his way over to the rise where Jake had pulled up.

"Might be trouble," Jake explained as he offered his brother a rifle. "Look, whatever you do, don't start shooting and spook the herd. I'm going to send Gene back to patrol with you. Do what he tells you, and everything'll be fine."

"I'd feel better if you came back yourself, Jake."

"I would, too," Jake confessed. "But trouble isn't apt to wait for me to make my way around to the others."

Jericho nodded his understanding, and Jake resumed his ride. He armed Gene and passed on Eddie's admonition.

"Sure, I know what's to be done," Gene replied. "Get along and tell Lenny. Pair him with Callahan and hurry back.

You're right about this west flank. It's certain to be our weak spot.''

After passing rifles on to Len Baxter and Ron Callahan, Jake swung around and collected Ty Wells.

"I don't see Albert," Jake muttered. "Isn't he watching the east flank?"

"Was a while back," Ty said, scratching his head. " 'Course, you never know with that fellow!"

"No, you don't," Jake agreed. "You better head on over and join Lenny and Callahan, Ty."

"I could go with you and scare up Albert," Ty suggested. "You can't be sure he's shirking this time. Could be the rustlers got him."

"Doesn't seem likely," Jake grumbled. "They've got the shadows working for them in the west. They'll have to drive the cattle off that way in the end. Our camp's to the east, too."

"So we wouldn't suspect 'em hitting us there, would we?" Ty asked. "If it was me, I wouldn't knock on a man's front door if I aimed to steal his gold. No, sir. I'd sneak in through the back window."

"It's a thought," Jake admitted. "Come along then, Ty. Let's have a look."

Jake led the way past the grazing longhorns, swinging first east and then south. There wasn't a trace of Albert, but Ty thought he spied a horse over the next rise.

"Want me to have a closer look?" Ty asked.

"No!" Jake barked. "Be a fine place for a bushwhacker, that slope. Ride to camp and fetch the others."

"You aim to stand guard all alone?" Ty asked.

"I can shoot just fine," Jake assured his young friend. "And you'll be back in a hurry, won't you?"

"Sure will," Ty promised, kicking his horse into a gallop.

As Ty sped toward the camp, Jake drew out his Sharps and cradled it in his arms. He'd never been much good shooting from the back of a horse. Animals tended to be skittish around firearms, and few held their riders anything close to steady.

"Come on, Ty," Jake whispered when he spotted a figure crawling along the side of the nearby hill. "Hurry."

The raiders' first shots struck the rocky earth a hundred yards from Jake. He knew they weren't meant to kill or maim. No, the raiders wanted to startle the herd, incite a stampede.

"Have to do better'n that!" Jake howled. He took up a trail song, half yelling the tune. The noise served to mute the rifle shots.

"Hurry, Ty," Jake pleaded again when the frustrated raiders mounted their horses and started toward him in earnest.

"Yawwwhaah!" they screamed, charging.

Now the cattle began to surge northward. Jake nudged his way south and waited for the first raider to enter rifle range. The Sharps was deadly at three hundred feet, and some said it could kill from as far away as a mile. Jake had never tried. He couldn't see that far away, so he didn't see how it mattered.

The first rustler closed in ever closer. He fired off a six-shot Colt revolver, and the cattle began scrambling away to the north. Jake held his breath, chambered a cartridge and fired. The explosion nearly knocked him from Bailey, but he hung on. The rustler fell back against his horse's rump and rolled off into the dust.

"Yawwwhaah!" the remaining thieves hollered.

Jake tried to reload, but Bailey refused to allow it. Only the prompt arrival of Ty, Eddie, and Si saved him. All three fired off pistols, and the rustlers turned away.

"They're going to slice off a quarter of the herd," Eddie muttered as he waved Jake along. Ty, Jordy, and Tip followed. Together the five cowboys managed to recover most of the longhorns, and Eddie dropped one of the raiders with a well-placed shot through the head.

Around on the opposite side, Gene continued to hold the west flank in check. The trail-weary cattle had refused to join the stampede, and the pair of would-be thieves who approached from the shadows were easily driven off.

It seemed to Jake that they had managed pretty well. The

bulk of the herd remained under their control, and none of the cowboys had been hurt.

"We would have cut 'em to pieces if Lofland had been here!" Ty hollered.

"Sure," Eddie mumbled. "Only he wasn't. Where's Wash anyhow? And Albert?"

"I don't know," Jake confessed. "I thought maybe they were back at camp."

"Wash was there earlier," Eddie noted, "but when we set off, he'd already disappeared. I left Jordy and Josh to watch the camp."

"Thanks," Jake said, sighing. "What now?"

"Somebody's got to get the cows back," Ty declared.

"Sure," Eddie agreed. "Not us, though, and not tonight. I've got no talent for riding strange country in the dark, and we've still got a herd to protect."

"Maybe Josh has some dinner ready," Jake suggested.

"Best we relieve the watch and send them along in first," Eddie declared. "They can come back and relieve us afterward."

Jake nodded his agreement. He and Ty spelled Gene and Jer. Si and Eddie rode over to replace Len and Callahan.

They slowly patrolled the fringe of the herd half an hour or so before riders approached from the north.

"It's us!" Colonel Dunlap announced as Jake slid the Sharps out of his saddle scabbard.

"Colonel!" Jake howled. "Glad you're back."

"I suspect you are," Colonel Dunlap said, leading his horse over. "Left Lofland and Wash to patrol up the way. Your brothers will be along to spell you shortly, Jacob Henry. Now, tell me about it."

"I guess it wasn't much of a fight," Jake confessed. "Mostly we just held our ground and ran the raiders off. They got some stock, but not many."

"Lost three men for their trouble, too," Duncan observed.

"One shot clean through the head. Second one in the chest.

A third got himself tangled up in the herd and stomped properly.''

"I didn't know about that one," Jake said, sighing. "Two were shot, huh? Dead?"

"About as dead as a man ever gets, son."

"I hit a man, but I wasn't sure I killed him," Jake said, shuddering. "Eddie dropped the other one."

"Colonel, it was a close thing," Ty observed. "Eddie and Jake saved our hides, passing out the rifles like they did. I sort of expected Wash to join in, though."

"He rode to McAlester's for help," Duncan explained.

"Took his buddy Albert along, too, I suppose," Ty grumbled.

"Wasn't he with you?" the colonel asked. "I assigned him to the watch myself. He sure didn't ride to McAlester's."

"Somebody ought to talk to that fellow," Ty declared. "He would have left the whole east flank naked to those raiders."

"Time we had a serious talk," Duncan growled. "You two head back now and get something to eat. We're apt to be up half the night, patrolling, and tomorrow we'll be chasing the thieves. I'll watch the herd myself until your brothers get here, Jake."

"Yes, sir," Jake said, turning Bailey south.

"That Albert!" Ty complained as he followed. "If the colonel doesn't chase him off, I believe I will!"

14

Morning found the entire crew exhausted. Jake had passed most of the night on guard against the raiders' return, and what scant rest he found was between midnight and dawn. The others weren't much better. The younger men were on edge, and the slightest trifle set them off like powder kegs.

"We can't take to the trail like this, Colonel," Eddie declared. "An outfit has to work together. These fellows are at each others' throats."

"We weren't going north anyway," Duncan grumbled. "We have a chore to tend first."

"You mean going after the raiders, don't you?" Jake asked.

"I do!" the colonel barked. "Nobody's ever stole anything off me and got away with it. It's a poor time for them to start now."

"Uncle John, Marty Albert's missing, too," Wash noted. "We ought to have a look for him first."

"He could be hurt," Josh added.

"More likely he ran out on us when those thieves hit," Eddie said, spitting. "Never was worth his feed."

"Still, we ought to look," Doc agreed.

"Time we did somethin' about those rustlers, too," Gene declared, motioning toward the flats where three buzzards were turning slow circles over a dark object.

"We didn't shoot anybody out that way," Eddie said, growing pale. "I dropped my man half a mile farther north."

"Mine was closer to the herd," Jake added.

"The other fellow was way up north," Colonel Duncan said, frowning. "Probably we've got some cows killed."

"That or something else," Lofland said, buckling his gun belt. "I need a couple of men to go with me, Colonel."

"Jake?" Eddie asked.

"Let me grab my Sharps," Jake said, turning. He didn't have the slightest inclination to ride out there, but who else was there? Jer? Jordy?

"I had you two in mind," Lofland confessed.

They walked together to the remuda and saddled their horses. Then Lofland led the way east and north to where the buzzards were flying. By the time the three riders reached the spot, the birds had settled atop the dark mound. Lofland charged, howling, and the birds slapped their wings in defiance. Only when the gunman fired his pistol would they leave.

"It's a man," Jake declared from fifty feet away.

"You can stay back if you want," Lofland said, continuing. "Ain't much I've not seen."

It must have been particularly awful, though, for Lofland swung off his horse and vomited.

"Ride back and tell the colonel we've found Albert," Lofland hollered.

Eddie and Jake exchanged sick looks. Jake then turned back toward the camp. Eddie drew out a bowie knife and dismounted. It wasn't much as shovels went, but it would suffice. Jake left his companions to bury the corpse.

"I knew he wouldn't just ride off," Wash remarked when Jake passed on the news to the others. "Never had a chance, riding out there alone and unarmed. I don't guess you thought to get him a rifle, did you, Jake Wetherby?"

"I'd say that was your responsibility, Wash," the colonel growled. "Anyhow, he's dead. We've got other troubles to deal with."

"We're sure going after 'em now," Wash declared. "We owe it to Marty."

"Like the colonel said, he's dead," Gene argued. "Those raiders won't be hangin' around, not knowin' they killed a man. Let's grab up our strays and get on along."

"We're not going anywhere just yet," Colonel Duncan insisted. "I want four men riding guard at a time. Another four can get some sleep."

"And the rest?" Jake asked.

"Go after the thieves," Duncan explained. "Wash, you want to head up that batch?"

"You know I'm little use with firearms, Uncle John," Wash said, nervously edging his way behind Gene Stuart.

"Me, neither," Callahan said. "I'll sure take the herd in hand, though, Colonel."

"You can't send the youngsters out there, Colonel," Doc Trimble argued.

"You sure can't," Lofland agreed as he rode up. "It's for me to do. How many hands can you spare to go along?"

"Two," Duncan said, frowning. "Three if Wash pulls a watch."

"Four could be enough," Lofland declared. "If it's the right four."

"I'd guess I'm the most experienced myself," Colonel Duncan said, sighing.

"Pardon me for saying it, Colonel, but you're past your hard riding days," Lofland argued. "Besides, you've got all the papers on the herd. If something were to happen . . ."

They all froze a moment. No one believed Wash capable of directing the drive.

"I'll go," Eddie said, frowning. "But I insist Gene stay with the herd. You'll need somebody who knows what to do."

"Tip should mind the horses," the colonel declared. "Jordy and Len are too young. Besides, they're the best ropers in the bunch. Ty?"

"I'll do as you figure best, Colonel," Ty replied.

"No, Colonel, I'm the one to go," Jake argued. "You know I can handle a rifle. I judge I've got a year on Ty here easy."

"There are your two," Duncan told Lofland. "You best pick the other yourself."

"I don't know I care to haul a beardless boy along," Lofland grumbled. "We can get by, the three of us."

"You'd be better off with four, though," Jericho argued. "I'll go."

"No!" Jake objected.

"Jake, you know I can shoot a rifle near as good as you can, and skinny like I am, I don't make much of a target. You can't let Jordy go, and Si wouldn't be any help. He'd be so busy studying the ill omens, he'd never get past McAlester's."

"He's only seventeen," Jake complained to the colonel.

"Older than you were when we first rode to the Brazos," Duncan noted.

"You'll be there to see I don't get myself shot up," Jericho told Jake.

"Sure," Jake admitted. But he'd never been any good at keeping anybody alive. Not friends. Not his mother. Not his father.

"Get your horse saddled, Jer," Lofland urged. "We won't catch anybody jawing in camp."

They paused only long enough to collect extra cartridges, caps, and bullets. Doc Trimble filled a provision bag, and Colonel Duncan sketched out a map where he'd drive the herd in case the pursuit dragged on past two days.

"It will, most likely," Lofland declared. "These sort of rats always hole up. They've got cows to sell, though, and that helps some."

"Some," Duncan agreed. "Not much."

Lofland led the way south from the herd.

"South?" Jake asked. "I thought they'd head north toward the markets. They have to sell our stock, don't they?"

"Lots of mouths to feed along this trail, Jake," Lofland noted. "I got a slight edge on you boys, too. You didn't get a look at the dead ones."

"No," Jake agreed. "You recognized them?"

"Just one fellow," Lofland explained. "Was missing a couple of fingers. Big man with a stupid grin on his face."

"The one that pulled the knife back at Boggy Depot?" Jake asked.

"I spied a couple of other familiar faces trailing us two days back," Lofland continued. "I'd guess they're the ones that hit us."

"Wouldn't it be better to find a trail and track 'em?" Eddie asked.

"Oh, I figure they wasted hours losing their trail in rocks and such," Lofland explained. "We'll cut 'em off down the trail."

"Get in behind them, you mean," Jer said.

"It's the best way," Lofland insisted. "Strike hard, fast, and sudden. Shoot the fools down before they have a chance to fire back."

"How will you be certain they're the right ones?" Jericho asked.

"I suppose we could let you ride out and ask," Lofland growled. "Might be we can tell when we see 'em driving our cows along."

"You can't argue much with that for proof," Eddie agreed. "What if they don't have the animals with 'em?"

"Don't see any point to troubling them in that case," Lofland replied. "No matter what the colonel says, my business is getting the cattle back. Those fellows are sure to get themselves killed anyhow before long. They cheat each other at cards, and they're stupid. You don't survive this country that way."

Jake thought that was probably true. Still, he would have felt more secure trailing the thieves. Falling on a batch of riders from ambush, with no proof they were the right ones, had a sour taste about it. As for cattle, they weren't the only ones to move longhorns along the Shawnee Trail.

"I don't care what Lofland says, either," Eddie told Jake. "I'm not shootin' anybody in the back. My pa was an outlaw and a no-account, but he always faced fellows head-on."

"He didn't get too old, either, did he?" Lofland called.

"Man's got good ears," Jake said, laughing. "He seems to know his business, too. I believe I'll follow his lead."

They rode steadily south most of the morning. That afternoon Lofland led the way west toward a high ridge overlooking the trail. From there they could study the country north and south for twenty miles in all directions.

"There," Lofland said, pointing to a small herd of cattle being coaxed south by seven riders.

"Seven?" Eddie gasped. "I didn't figure there'd be so many."

"Still want to face 'em head-on, do you?" Lofland asked.

"I won't shoot a man in the back," Eddie vowed.

"Then I wish I'd asked young Josh along," Lofland said, spitting. "Doc maybe. They'd be more use in the sort of fight that's coming."

Eddie bristled, but he held his anger inside. Lofland continued to study the rustlers. As they grew closer, the gunman cracked a smile.

"All right," he told his companions. "Listen good. They're turning onto the road. Jake, you and your brother slip down along the road and hide in that stand of oaks yonder. Sight in your rifles, and open on 'em when they close to a hundred feet."

"All right," Jake agreed.

"Now, Eddie, you and me have the touchy part. We have to ride down and peel the riders off the herd. You can shoot 'em if your conscience won't trouble you, or just set 'em to running. Once they're gone, Jake, you and Jer there get mounted and start the cattle north. We'll follow once we've tended the riders."

"Seems simple enough," Jake declared.

"Won't be," Lofland assured them. "You'll have time to think on it. Isn't the same, shooting men that way. You do it quick, it's an instinct. Just a man's hunger to survive. Try to think on it that way, and you'll fare better. Just remember that if you drop the first two, the odds'll favor us living to see trail's end."

"Sure," Jake agreed.

Jake knew Lofland was right about the killing, though. As he and Jericho rode down to the oaks, he tried to erase the image of the raider he'd shot the night before. In spite of the dust and haze, the man's features were permanently etched in Jake's brain.

"I've shot plenty of animals," Jericho said when they reached the trees. "Can't be so different."

"Can," Jake insisted. "Is."

They tied their horses securely and took shelter behind a limestone boulder. The raiders approached slowly. Their bloodshot eyes and dusty faces told of an equally exhausting night.

"I'll take the one on the right," Jericho said, breathing deeply.

"The one on the sorrel?" Jake asked.

"That's the one," Jericho replied. "He's mine."

"I'll take the one on the paint, then," Jake said, studying the man. There was something faintly familiar about him. As he closed the range, Jake knew what it was. This was the big farmer who'd tripped him that night at the depot saloon.

"When do we do it, Jake?" Jericho asked anxiously. The younger Wetherby was growing impatient. His rifle trembled.

"Just when they reach the edge of the road," Jake suggested. "Another ten feet."

"That close?" Jer asked.

"Important thing's to hit your target, Jer."

"Sure," Jericho said, coughing.

Jake felt his fingers sweat. He had to fight for air.

Steady up! he told himself. This is no time to panic.

Jericho fired first. The rifle split the air with its distinctive crack. Jake saw his target turn and glance back. He fired a split second later. The Sharps spit its deadly projectile out of the oaks. It whined through the air and struck the raider just behind the right ear.

"Lord," Jake gasped as the man's head exploded.

"I got mine, too," Jericho said, fighting to reload his rifle. The young man's forehead was beading up with perspiration, and his eyes appeared hollow.

"Leave the rest to me," Jake said as he slid a fresh bullet

in place. Already Lofland was leading Eddie down the ridge, and the surviving raiders turned that way. Jake filled his sights with a slender rider whose raven-colored hair fell across his forehead and nearly covered his eyes. With a sour sadness engulfing his whole being, Jake stared at the raider and pressed the trigger. This time the bullet struck its victim in the chest and tore him from his saddle. The corpse was swallowed by a tempest of dust thrown up by his companions' horses.

"I can't seem to—" Jer cried when Jake turned to his brother.

"Forget about it, Jer," Jake urged. "Let's mount up and collect the longhorns. Leave the rest of those fellows to Lofland."

15

The sudden attack had sent the longhorns fleeing northward. They were already scattering when Jake and Jericho arrived.

"Yah!" Jake yelled as he circled around, cutting off the wayward animals. "Yah!"

Jericho split away and cut off a pair heading west. He was driving the wayward steers back to the others when Jake saw the rustlers.

"Jer, watch out!" Jake shouted as he abandoned the cattle and drew out his rifle.

Stan Lofland and Eddie Stuart had driven the thieves well westward, but two had eluded them. They were now charging toward the road.

Jericho saw them, too, but not before the pistol-wielding raiders were able to open fire.

"Jer!" Jake howled as his brother rolled off his horse and fell to the dusty ground.

With rare cool Jake steadied his bay and readied the Sharps. He took deadly aim and fired. The thieves were then less than fifteen feet away, and the impact of the bullet lifted the foremost rider off his horse and slammed him against the rocky surface of the road.

The second raider swerved away. A rifle cracked off in the distance, and he, too, fell dead.

"Jer?" Jake called, urging the bay on toward his brother. "Jer?"

"Jake?" Jericho called, sitting up. His face was pale as a ghost, and he hugged a bloody left hand against his chest.

120

"Dear Lord," Jake said, hopping down from his horse. "How bad is it?"

"Be a handicap strumming the guitar," Jericho said, wincing as he displayed his hand. The left ring finger was a mangled mess. Aside from considerable bleeding, though, Jericho seemed well enough.

"I thought you were dead, sure," Jake said, pulling out a kerchief and binding the wound.

"They came on us so quick," Jer said, growing faint.

"Happens that way," Jake observed. "Good thing Lofland and Eddie weren't too far off. Saved us both, dropping that second fellow."

"The cattle?" Jer mumbled.

"Oh, they're just fine," Jake said, staring at the longhorns milling about near the edge of the road. "Guess they got used to the shooting."

"We'd better get them on back," Jericho said, trembling.

"We will," Jake assured his brother. "Here now, that too tight?"

"Feels better," Jericho noted. "You took up the wrong calling, Jake. Should've been a doctor."

"Hush," Jake urged.

By then Eddie had arrived to take the cattle in hand. Lofland followed a bit later.

"Can he ride?" the gunman asked Jake.

"He'll have to," Jake replied. "I don't see any wagons handy."

"Tie him on, son," Lofland advised. "Then go on ahead with him. Stuart and I'll follow with the stock."

"Sure," Jake agreed.

As they hurried north, Jake realized how fast it had all happened. Only that morning he and Jer had sat sleepy-eyed beside the cook fire while the colonel vowed to punish the rustlers. It was just mid-afternoon now, and they had dealt with the thieves. It seemed the ride south had been a blur. The return trip dragged on into an eternity.

"How's the hand?" Jake called out from time to time.

"Hurts," Jericho replied at first.

"It's bleeding again," he added later.

Twice Jake paused to tighten the bandage.

"Doc'll be taking that finger off, won't he?" Jericho finally asked.

"It's just about off on its own," Jake confessed. "Yeah, I suspect it's got to go, Jer."

"Be interesting, come my wedding day," Jericho said, forcing a grin onto his face. "Bride'll have a tough time slipping a ring onto a stump."

"Figure on marrying anybody real soon?" Jake asked.

"No, but we're not all of us Wetherbys going to pass our days chasing cows and shooting outlaws."

"Trust not," Jake said, shuddering as the faces of the dead men flashed through his mind.

"It eats at you, doesn't it, Jake? The killing."

"I guess if you do it often enough, you get used to it," Jake declared. "Lofland doesn't seem much bothered."

"I hope I never get to where killing a man doesn't trouble me some."

"Yeah," Jake agreed as he remounted Bailey. "Me, too."

Those last few miles Jake spoke less often. Exhaustion and anxiety were beginning to take a toll. He could hear Jericho yelp whenever his horse landed, and Jake wound up leading his wounded brother's mount north. When the gray mist rising from the Duncan herd finally came into his view, Jake whispered a prayer of deliverance.

"Jer?" Josh cried as Jake pulled up to Doc Trimble's wagon.

"He's hurt some," Jake announced as he dismounted. "Help me get him—"

The words were wasted. Josh and Si were already sliding Jericho off his horse. Doc hurried over, sized up the situation, and ordered a brand heated.

"What are you going to do?" Jer whined.

"Only thing I know," Doc said, applying a comforting hand to Jericho's shoulder. "Got to take that finger off and seal the wound, boy. It's going to hurt some, but when we're finished, you'll heal up fine."

"Give or take a finger," Jericho muttered.

"Ah, you'll do fine with nine," Doc insisted. "I once saw a Crow Indian up north had only six. Three on each hand."

"He ever play a guitar?" Jericho asked.

"Nope, but then you're only learning. Man can learn to get by when he don't know any difference, I suspect."

"Can play as good as you, anyhow," Josh said, settling in alongside his brother as Doc cut away the binding.

"Peanut, maybe you ought to—" Jake began.

"No, let him stay," Jericho urged. "It's a comfort."

Jake nodded and set off past the wagon.

"Better get some sleep, Jacob Henry," Colonel Duncan advised. "You look done in."

"You didn't ask about the cows," Jake realized. "I—"

"I'll hear about it later," the colonel said, smiling faintly. "If it was anything bad, you would've said it straight out."

"Lofland and Eddie are bringing 'em along," Jake explained.

"Smart thing, hurrying your brother back," the colonel noted. "Wish there'd been a way to leave it to somebody else."

"Never is, though," Jake said, sighing. Jordy rushed over with a cold biscuit and some dried beef, but Jake couldn't eat. Instead he rolled out his blankets and tried to find some rest. It was an hour coming, but once he fell asleep, he didn't wake until dusk.

By then, of course, Eddie and Lofland had returned with the stolen cattle. When Jake roused himself and stumbled over to the cook fire, he discovered himself a hero.

"Should've seen that boy, Colonel," Lofland boasted. "Sat there cool as an icehouse, drawing a bead on those rascals. Dropped two from the oaks and another on the road. Pure waste, sending the rest of us. Jake, there, would have settled with all seven."

"Three?" Jordy cried. "You got three of 'em, Jake?"

"I don't find much in it to brag on," Jake said, accepting a bowl of stew from Josh. "Truth is, it tears at me."

"That passes," the colonel declared.

"Does it?" Jake asked, turning to Lofland.

"Pray it doesn't," the gunman answered. "It never ought to get like respectable work. Won't if you're lucky."

As Jake ate his stew, he glanced over to the wagon. Jericho lay there, resting.

"He's all right, isn't he?" Jake whispered to Josh.

"Doc gave him some whiskey," Josh explained. "Got him quieted down.'Fore that he was hollering considerably."

"Don't worry after him," Doc advised. "He'll mend just fine. I've seen plenty of fingers and toes shot off—arms and legs, too. Got a stump myself, you know. I know what's needed. He'll ride in the wagon a day or two in case there's fever. But he's going to perk up by the time we reach the Arkansas. Trust me to know."

"He should've stayed here," Jake grumbled.

"Oh, he wanted to go," Si argued. "He's the one with the hunger to see the next hillside, Jake. Wade into trouble. You know that. Besides, he's got himself a curiosity to show the gals now."

Jordy managed a grin. Jake remained somber.

Colonel Duncan held the herd idle the following day, insisting the stolen cattle merited consideration. Jake knew it was Jericho who earned the favor. Or perhaps himself. The colonel gave Jake and Eddie most of the day off, and they slept a good deal of it away.

Once the drive did resume, they made good progress. They managed to cross the Canadian in fine fashion and press on northward. Daily parties of Texas-bound settlers passed by, and one night the colonel made his camp among the Creek Indians.

"Now here's a pleasant surprise," Wash said afterward. "No tolls."

It didn't quite make up for the disappointment they felt upon reaching the Arkansas the final week of June. The river was flooded right out of its banks, and there wasn't a prayer of crossing.

"Happens this way," a Cherokee trader camped on the

banks explained. "Rains upriver. Be fordable in a couple of days."

"How long?" the colonel cried. "Two days?"

"Three maybe."

"There has to be a passable ford downstream," Duncan argued.

"Not less'n a week's ride," the Cherokee insisted. "Only thing to do's sit here and wait it out."

That was the only thing to do, but it didn't keep the colonel from complaining.

"Might as well try to rope the wind!" Ty said as he and Jake rode night watch together. "A river's only goin' to fall when it does. No sooner. All the swearin' in tarnation won't hurry it along."

Jake had little reason to curse the delay. The horses enjoyed the rest, and Jericho responded by regaining his feet.

"It's far too solemn around here, Jer," Jake told him that first night on the Arkansas. "How about giving us a tune?"

"I don't know that I can hold on to anything just yet," Jericho said, staring at his bandaged hand.

"I only know one way to find out," Josh said, bringing the guitar. "Try it."

Jericho cradled the guitar in his damaged hand. He hesitated to use the fingers of his left hand to mark the chords, but he strummed along with his right pretty well.

"I don't know what to play," Jer said, gazing up sadly.

"One of Ollie's tunes," Len suggested. "Somethin' to make us all less lonely."

Jericho strummed a few moments before managing a tune. Then, without thinking, he touched the fingers of his left hand to the strings and formed chords.

In the beginning there was only the music. It was a little rough, but it smoothed out as Jer regained his confidence. Then Jordy took up the words, and the others joined in.

"Lonesome wind, blow me home," they sang. "Where the roses bloom brightest, and Jenny is smiling. Lonesome wind, blow me home. Back to Texas where the sun shines and the weather is fair."

It wasn't the most cheerful of songs, but it mirrored their feelings. And afterward they sang "Wild Women" and "Donkey Foot"—neither of which had a serious line to it.

"Glad you fellows are enjoying yourselves," Colonel Duncan grumbled when he returned from circling the herd. "We'll be paying for this delay next week when the price falls at market."

"Ah, Colonel, it rains everywhere," Ty argued. "Don't you figure the Canadian's swollen, too? Red River's likely worse. Those herds farther south are sure to be slowed, too. And when we do cross, the stock'll be stronger. We won't lose many swimming over."

"He's got a point, Colonel," Jake noted.

"Guess he does," Duncan admitted. He then climbed off his horse and joined in the singing.

The following morning the river had dropped to the point a man could swim his horse across, and Colonel Duncan rode out to visit Fort Gibson. The army had left the post, but the Cherokees had taken it over. The cowboys passed the day washing clothes, mending tack, hunting rabbits in the hollows, and hooking fish at the river.

"The Cherokees say there are thirty-pound catfish here," Josh declared. "I plan to hook myself one."

"Just see it isn't the other way around, Peanut," Jake urged. "No fish gets that big without learning a trick or two along the way."

They had poor success at first, but when Jericho came along with his guitar, the fish virtually leaped out of the water. Jake snagged a ten-pounder, and little Josh hooked one half again that big.

"Must be the music," Josh declared.

"Just how do you mean that?" Jericho growled. "Don't figure those fish tried to kill themselves, do you?"

"No," Jake said, laughing.

"They were plum charmed out of the river," Josh added. "Fried catfish is going to taste mighty fine tonight."

"Better'n more dried beef," Jericho agreed. "I almost

hope some steer drowns tomorrow so we can have fresh meat.''

"Don't let the colonel hear you talk that way," Jake warned. "We'd like as not be eating you, Jer.''

"Nope," Josh argued. "He's way too stringy. Nobody could make a meal out of him. Not even Doc.''

Colonel Duncan returned from Fort Gibson with fresh shot and powder, and the crew passed the balance of the day making cartridges.

"Expect a lot of trouble up north?" Jake asked afterward

"It's only smart to be prepared," Duncan explained.

The third morning the river dropped enough to get the wagon across, and by early afternoon Colonel Duncan started the first cattle over. The river remained wide, and deep in places, and the current was swift. The cowboys were well-practiced in the art of rescuing snagged steers now, though, and all but two hundred were gotten safely across when night fell. The others were nudged over the following morning, and once again the drive resumed its northward march.

"On to St. Louis!" Eddie yelled as he circled the herd.

"Yah!" Gene added as he helped stir the cattle. "Yah!"

"Guess you aren't as eager to get there, eh?" Jake called to the animals. "Faster to the stew pot!"

The animals seemed to moan a reply, and Jake shook his head.

"Been trailing these critters so long I almost think I can talk to 'em," Jake told his horse. "Guess it's time we finished this business.''

Bailey snorted a reply, and Jake found himself laughing.

"Wild women," he sang.

Gene took up the tune farther back, and soon the song echoed back and forth across the herd. It gave the horses a lighter pace, and it cast a somber shroud from the crew.

16

They camped that night beside an old mission near where the Verdigris River flowed into the Arkansas.

"Another river to cross," Wash Duncan grumbled.

"Oh, it's nothin' compared to the Arkansas," Eddie observed. "We'll get ourselves across tomorrow easy."

Meanwhile Jake and his brothers took advantage of a small chapel. Although their prayers were silent, Jake knew most concerned Jericho and the dangers left to face on the way north.

"Lord, watch over us," Jake whispered after his brothers left. "Keep us clear of harm's shadow."

The mission had been built to minister to the needs of Indians, but there were a number of whites there as well.

"Mostly trail orphans," a Cherokee woman explained. "We send some south when families stop by. Once in a while somebody's lost a child, and they're grateful to take in one of our little strays."

Jake couldn't help feeling kinship for the orphans. The cowboys invited the youngsters out to the river for a swim that afternoon. Colonel Duncan offered a lame steer, and Doc Trimble barbecued the animal. The mission folk enjoyed the feast, and afterward Jericho entertained them with a song or two.

"It's a sad thing," the colonel observed later when their guests had left. "People leaving their kids behind like that."

"I thought their folks were dead," Jake said, frowning.

"Some are," the colonel admitted, "but most were left because they got to be a bother."

"We could add a boy or two to the outfit, Colonel," Eddie suggested.

"Got too many fool children along as it is," the colonel complained. "But when we leave tomorrow, cut out four or five cows for 'em. Cows, mark you. Steers wouldn't do much good."

"Sir?" Eddie asked.

"Some of those little ones look in need of milk."

"Yes, sir," Eddie readily agreed.

Once across the Verdigris, the Shawnee Trail followed the Grand River northeast toward the Missouri border. Almost daily now parties of emigrants trudged by in their rickety wagons. There were several freighters hauling goods from Missouri into the Nations, too. Colonel Duncan tended to give both groups some distance. He more readily accepted the hospitality of Cherokee farmers and horse traders.

"Wouldn't hurt to swap out some of the mounts," Tip told the colonel. "Stock's better here, and you might get a better price than up north."

"Seems wise, Colonel," Lofland agreed. "We get hit by road agents, we've only got two or three ponies up to the hard work it would take to catch 'em."

So once again Tip and the colonel sat down with the Cherokees and traded. Jake considered Bailey still fit, and he insisted on retaining the animal. Some of the other men kept their work horses, too, but the spare animals were swapped off for fitter stock.

Jordy tried to entice some of the younger Cherokees into racing Buster, but the Indians recognized the stallion's fine lines and declined.

"Guess nobody's eager to give you his horse, little brother," Jake observed. "Have to wait till we head back into Choctaw territory."

"Those Choctaws have good memories," Jericho cackled. "You won't find them lining up to have a go at Buster, either."

"May be just as well," Jordy said, grinning. "I've still got a welt or two left from that whip!"

By the first of July the Duncan outfit reached Cabin Creek, a shallow stream along which the Cherokees had built a small settlement. A worried John Duncan assembled the men at dinner to pass on news he'd picked up from the inhabitants.

"There's a bad batch of men operating in this country," he explained. "Bluejackets, they're called. Deserters from the army mostly. They haunt the border strip between here and Missouri. Sometimes they even drift over into the southern part of Kansas Territory."

"You figure they'll hit the herd, Uncle John?" Wash asked.

"Could be," Duncan replied. "They prefer freighters, but a thousand head of prime longhorns would be a tempting target."

"What do you want us to do?" Jake asked.

"Double up when you ride night watch," the colonel declared. "Keep your guns handy, too. Sleep with 'em. Be alert. You spy something, one of you ride back and rouse the camp."

"And the other?" Eddie asked.

"Stay and watch," Duncan instructed. "Listen. Don't do anything to give yourself away. Just study the matter. And when we ride out, let us know what we're up against."

"Sounds easy enough," Gene said, shrugging his shoulders.

"Won't be if they're serious about hitting us," Lofland argued. "Just stay out of sight and hold your water. A man panics in a tight spot, he's apt to get killed."

Jake nodded, as did most of the others. When he and Gene rode night guard, he tried to take all the advice to heart. The sky overhead was clear of clouds, though, and moonlight gave any would-be raider a clear picture of the herd and its guards.

"Gives us a fair idea of who or what might be comin'," too," Gene noted when Jake complained. "Don't worry. They'd be more apt to come when they have a better edge."

That notion didn't provide Jake with much solace. He kept alert for any trace of intruders, but the night passed rather peacefully. Except for a bawling steer that got itself snagged in a ravine, there was hardly a sound.

The next day Jake was up at first light, as were most of the others.

"Seems like you boys can't wait to get on north," Doc observed as he sliced strips of ham and threw them into a hot skillet. "Must not take to this place."

"Don't take to outlaws, and that's for certain," Ty declared. "Sooner we get along, the better I'll like it."

The rest of the crew agreed. For once John Dunlap had no need of urging the men to rouse the herd. They were yelling the stock across Cabin Creek before the sun got itself properly past the eastern horizon.

That second day of July proved as uneventful as the first, though. From time to time riders happened along, but each one rode swiftly and with purpose. There were no hangarounds or overfriendly visitors.

Unfortunately the weather turned hostile that evening. Dark storm clouds choked the sky and swallowed the stars. For once there wasn't one glimmer of moonlight.

"Raiders' weather," Gene observed when he and Jake again shared the late evening watch.

"Oh, I don't mind the dark," Jake insisted. "It's like a cloak that hides you from your enemies."

"Hides them, too," Gene argued.

"You need to see a fellow to know he's there?" Jake asked. "I don't. I can hear and smell him, and so can the cattle. We'd know we had visitors, but they wouldn't see us. I call that an edge for us."

Jake had scarcely spoken the words when the cattle along a small stream fifty yards away began to stir. First there was a deep moan or two. Then one batch of ten or so scrambled northward.

"Trouble," Jake observed, swinging his horse around. "Coming along?"

"Somebody ought to rouse the camp," Gene suggested.

"Best we check out the trouble first," Jake urged. "Could be a coyote."

Jake eased his way around the herd. Bailey was a reliable mount, and he kept clear of the deadly nest of horns twenty feet away. Gene followed somewhat reluctantly. He was close enough to help, though.

"There," Jake whispered, pointing toward the stream. He could hear feet splashing through the shallows.

"Here's one now," a voice called.

"I see her, Tom. Throw your rope over her."

Jake felt his muscles tense as he closed the distance.

"I'm ridin' for the camp," Gene called, turning away.

Jake waved him along and took stock of the situation. He couldn't detect horses. What madness was this, creeping into a herd of longhorns on foot?

"Who's there?" the first voice shouted then.

Jake halted Bailey and waited for a shot to mark the intruder's position. None came. Instead the second voice urged retreat.

"What in . . ." Jake muttered. One voice creaked and cracked like a half-grown boy. The other was girlish high-pitched.

"All right there!" Jake shouted. "Who are you?"

The would-be thieves splashed around the creek a minute before rushing up the bank. Jake drew out his rifle and searched for a target. He found none. One of the intruders tried to drag a cow along, but the stubborn longhorn refused to budge.

"Fool cow," the young voice cried, stomping on the hard ground as if that would hurry the animal. It didn't.

"Stop!" Jake shouted. "Hold up there. I've got a rifle!"

"Lordy, Tom!" the cracking voice cried.

Before Jake could approach any closer, a yellow streak of lightning tore the sky overhead. Jake caught a momentary glimpse of two shadowy figures, but that was all. The thunder that followed disturbed the herd, and Bailey instinctively backed away.

"Tom?" the older intruder screamed. "Tommy, where've you gone?"

Before Jake could react, a gust of icy wind swept across

the land, stinging his face with sharp rain pellets. The long-horns turned in a flash and rushed down the bank of the stream and on across to the opposite side. Jake fought to settle Bailey as the animals raced past. Then he heard a high-pitched scream that sent icy slivers up his spine.

"Tommy!" a slightly deeper voice called. A second piercing scream followed shortly.

Jake's first urge was to race in and investigate, but that wasn't possible. The milling cattle weren't about to allow a horse to pass amongst them, and he had no idea as to whether other raiders were close by. Only when Gene returned with Stan Lofland, the colonel, and Si Garrett did Jake catch his breath.

"Size it up for me, Jake," Lofland said, drawing one of his twin revolvers. "Who is it? Where are they?"

"I don't know who," Jake explained, "but I only counted two voices. They didn't seem to have any company."

"Where are they?" Lofland asked.

"Down in the stream yonder," Jake replied. "There's a sea of cattle there just now."

"They on horseback?" Lofland asked.

"Don't think so, Mr. Lofland," Jake explained. "I didn't see or hear a hint of mounts. They sounded real young, too."

"A young man can kill you as certain as an old one," Lofland argued. "You're proof of that yourself, Jake."

"Jacob Henry, what do you figure we've got out there?" the colonel asked.

"I can't say for certain," Jake confessed, "but I'd guess maybe some boys off a wagon company or maybe from a nearby farm came in and tried to rope a cow. Now they've got themselves cut off by the herd."

"Didn't work out quite like they planned, huh?" the colonel asked.

"If that's what's down there," Lofland muttered. "Si, ride along back to camp and fetch a lantern. Jake, let's see if we can clear these cattle out of the way."

"At night?" Jake asked.

"Come on," Gene urged. "We've handled stock before after dusk, Jake."

"You don't know there aren't rifles aimed at us right now," Jake argued.

"Trust us to avenge your murder, Jake," Lofland said, laughing.

Gene nudged Jake's elbow, and the two of them moved down toward the cattle, whistling and slapping ropes against their knees. The longhorns reluctantly moved on along, abandoning the stream. Even before Si arrived with the lantern, Jake saw what they were after. A fresh flash overhead illuminated two odd lumps beside the stream.

"I see 'em, too," Gene mumbled. "Go slow, Jake. Wait for the lantern."

Jake did for a time. Then one of the shapes moved. An arm clawed at the sky, and Jake nudged Bailey ahead.

"Jake?" Gene called.

"One of 'em's moving," Jake explained.

He couldn't get a very clear idea of who the intruder was, but the shape was too small to be anyone very substantial. What passed for a voice managed nothing more than a shrill whine.

Jake dismounted and knelt beside the lumps. He touched the trembling hand and found it moist. A sickly sweet odor hung in the air.

"Who are you?" Jake whispered. "Where'd you come from?"

"Tom," the voice cried. "Tommy?"

Si happened along then with the lantern, and Gene directed him toward the stream. Si held the faint yellow swirl of light out as he rode closer. When it fell on the stream bed, Jake leaped back in horror. The figure beside him was barely recognizable. Its legs stuck out at crazy angles, and its middle was stomped and torn into a mass of raw meat. Two bright blue eyes stared up from what had once been a face.

"Tommy?" the bloody mouth whimpered.

The other lump was simply torn to pieces. Hooves and horns had pounded and torn a somewhat smaller body apart.

"Who are you?" Jake pleaded as he fought to keep his insides from exploding. "Who—"

The bloody arm made a final futile try to touch the sky. Then it fell, lifeless.

"Colonel?" Jake cried, turning toward his companions.

"Kids," Duncan growled. "Just kids."

"We should take them back to camp, have Doc take a look," Jake suggested. "Maybe he can—"

"They're past hope, son," Lofland declared, hopping off his horse. "Go along now, Jake, and watch the stock. Leave me to do what's needed here."

"Colonel?" Jake asked, searching for some sort of explanation. He needed to understand. Ached to.

"Resume your watch, Jacob Henry," Duncan ordered. "You can do those two no good now."

Jake continued to ride night watch with Gene, but neither of them spoke. The air had turned strangely cold, and even the sky exploding overhead failed to erase the specter of the bloody face back at the stream.

"Can't take it all to heart, Jake," Gene said when they gave over their watch and returned to camp. "It'll eat you alive."

"I can't help myself," Jake replied. "They weren't any bigger'n Josh. No bigger than my own peanut of a brother."

"They came to steal our stock," Gene pointed out. "Young or old, they got what they deserved."

After passing a restless night, Jake awoke to find the rest of the crew readying their horses.

"You let me sleep past breakfast?" Jake asked in dismay.

"You passed a pretty hard night," Doc Trimble explained. "We all thought you needed a little extra rest. Josh is down saddlin' your horse. He's been beggin' to work the herd some, and it seemed the right day to have him try."

"No," Jake argued. "There are thieves around, and—"

"He's ridin' with Lofland," Doc explained. "Don't figure he's in any danger there."

Jake shrugged his shoulders and accepted a plate of ham and biscuits. As he ate he tried to forget the nightmare that had plagued his sleep. The nightmare that had been real enough a few hours earlier.

Jake was riding beside Doc Trimble atop the cook wagon when a round-faced woman of thirty-five drove a two-wheeled cart up from the opposite direction.

"Howdy there!" she called.

"Howdy," Doc answered.

"You ain't seen a pair of little boys about, has you?" she asked. "Towheaded youngsters. Twelve and ten years old. Were wearin' overalls."

Jake's pale face answered her question, and before Doc could speak, the woman yelled to the gaggle of little ones following the wagon to seek shelter.

"You sent them, didn't you?" Doc asked.

"Lord, man, we had to eat our milk cow day before yesterday," the woman explained. "You've got a thousand critters here. You'd hardly miss one or two."

"The colonel would've given you a cow," Jake told her. "I would've paid for it myself."

"I look like the sort of woman begs charity off strangers?" she asked.

"No," Doc grumbled. "You just send your boys off to get themselves trampled."

"What?" she cried.

"They're dead, the both of them," Jake explained. "Wandered in among the longhorns and got run down. Didn't know who they were, so we buried them back up the way at a small stream."

"Dead?" she wailed.

"Made themselves a considerable mistake," Doc observed.

"Never should've gone in among those cows," the woman said, shaking her head.

"Never should've trusted a mother who'd send them out to steal," Doc argued. "Now get along with you, woman, before John Duncan finds out who you are. He hangs thieves."

"I hear you, mister," the woman said, whipping her mules into motion. The little ones raced after her.

"The graves!" Jake shouted. "Aren't you going to mark 'em?"

The woman didn't reply. Her eyes were on the trail southward.

17

Jake rejoined the other cowboys that same afternoon. His heart remained heavy, but as he settled into the trail routine, he gradually let the memory of the dead boys drift away.

Meanwhile, Stan Lofland was oddly active. He rode back and forth along the western fringe of the herd, keeping an eye on any and every rider who appeared. That northern stretch of the Indian Nations seemed to draw drifters and no-accounts like a peach blossom drew bees. Three hours shy of dusk Colonel Duncan ordered the herd halted.

"There's a good stretch of grass here," the colonel explained. "Creek to the north and east, too. Ought to be easy to defend."

Jake told himself Lofland wasn't the only one to take the bluejackets seriously. Duncan had a second reason for calling an early halt to the day's drive, though.

"There's a freight station just ahead," the colonel explained. "I'm expecting an answer to a letter I mailed from Texas. Should tell us if we've got a buyer for the herd."

This was news to Jake, who had expected all along they'd drive the cattle into St. Louis and sell them at auction. Colonel Duncan had another idea, though. When he reappeared just before supper, he drew Wash off to one side and spoke for several minutes. Then the colonel assembled the others.

"Men, I'm going to leave you this evening," Duncan explained. "I'm meeting some buyers up in Kansas Territory. We'll dicker some, and if all goes well, I'll have a deal made by the time you get the herd to Baxter's cabin."

"Where?" Jake asked.

"Baxter's half trader, half farmer," the colonel said, laughing. "Lives on Shawnee land in southern Kansas Territory. You can't miss his place. It's just across the border, and a good trail takes you right there."

"Any relation of yours, Lenny?" Josh asked.

"None I know of," Len replied. "I've got lots of cousins somewhere, though."

"Colonel, who's runnin' the outfit while you're gone?" Eddie asked.

They all dreaded the answer. And it was Wash who gave it.

"I am," the younger Duncan declared. "You just do your jobs like you have, and we won't have any trouble."

"He knows what to do," the colonel added. "Not much to it now. You're maybe a week away. By riding on, I hope to shorten our journey considerably. With a little luck we'll deliver the herd right at Baxter's and start back home."

That was news indeed! Jake studied the faces of his companions. They all seemed to brighten at the notion that trail's end was close at hand.

There was nevertheless some grumbling about taking orders from Wash, but Eddie summed it up best.

"What harm can he do in a week's time?"

They had their first taste the following morning. No sooner had the colonel left than Wash produced three jugs of corn liquor.

"Got 'em off a Cherokee trader," Wash explained. "Well? What do you say? They're for you, boys!"

"Drinkin' don't much go with cattle," Eddie complained.

"We're not driving the herd anywhere today," Wash insisted. "It's Independence Day! The Fourth of July!"

"Only Independence Day I ever celebrated was in March," Eddie objected. "Texas independence. I never heard of anybody celebratin' anything in July."

"American independence," Jake explained. "When the Declaration of Independence was signed in Philadelphia."

"Somebody's had schooling," Wash noted. "Anyhow, it

ould be unpatriotic not to have a drink to our great coun-
ry.''

"Doc, you ever heard of such foolishness?" Eddie asked.

"Seems to me if I can give up a leg for the nation, you
boys can give up a day's work," Doc barked. "Toss me one
of those jugs. I ain't above a sip."

Moments later the jugs were making their way from cowboy to cowboy. In half an hour Josh was heaving behind the
cook wagon. Tip and Jordy were snoring away down by the
remuda. Jake knew better than to take more than a taste, for
he'd had an encounter with frontier spirits before. Jer and
Si, on the other hand, were eager to have another adventure.
They were now waddling around like a pair of stewed ducks,
whining some of Ollie's bawdy tunes and trying to avoid
stumbling over their own feet.

Eddie and Gene were just slightly drunk, and Lofland had
kept Callahan, Len, and Ty out with him, guarding the herd.
As for Wash, he was passed out cold under the wagon.

"Some celebration!" Josh later told Jake. "I never been
so sick in all my life. I feel like somebody reached in and
pulled my insides out. I swear there's still wasps buzzing
around in my head!"

"This stuff's worse'n Brazos corn liquor," Jake declared.
"I don't know what they put into it, but I swear it'll take the
hide right off!"

"Sure will shine a spur up pretty, though," Gene observed.

"Just keep it clear of your boots," Jake advised. "Like
as not'll burn a hole right through the leather."

The one positive effect of the liquor was that they all slept
well for a change. In fact, they slept right through night guard
duty. Fortunately the cattle settled down peacefully, the skies
remained clear, and no raiders appeared.

When sunrise announced the fifth had arrived, more than
one cowboy awoke with a pounding head. Doc Trimble didn't
offer much sympathy. He clanged his big iron pot with a
heavy spoon, rousing them from their dreams. Then he of-

fered each two spoonfuls of the most awful-tasting concoction known to man.

"Lord, Doc, what is that?" Jer cried as he clutched his stomach.

"General cure-all," Doc explained. "Heals snakebite, grows hair, and empties out a man real fast."

They soon had their proof of the tonic's potency. Jericho grabbed a paper and headed for the nearby brush. He was followed by Si and Josh. In the end every single one of them headed for cover.

"Whew," Tip said, shaking his head. "Barely got my pants off before the flow commenced. Don't know if the cure's worth the medicine!"

Whether it sped the crew's recovery or not, Jake never was quiet certain. But the threat of a second dose squelched all complaint.

"Wash, you better get these boys mounted and start drivin' cattle!" Doc announced after meting out biscuits and coffee. "If your uncle gets to Baxter's and finds us still south, you'll have some fast talking ahead of you."

Wash appeared befuddled about what to say or do, though. He stood by, hoping the men would take it on themselves to saddle their horses, but no one appeared eager to begin.

"Come on, men," he finally growled. "Get mounted. We've got to move the herd along north."

"Who's leadin' us?" Eddie asked. "You want to change anybody around? Did last time, as I recollect."

"Marty's dead," Wash grumbled. "No, you all ride like you have been. It's worked pretty well so far. Long as we stay on the road, we'll get to Baxter's. I'll be up front, but all you need do is keep the herd on the trail."

"Sure," Eddie agreed. "Let's get to it, fellows."

"Keep an eye out for trouble today," Lofland warned. "We're still in bluejacket country."

If that hadn't been clear before, it was by mid-afternoon. Jake was riding right point as always, but he edged a hair closer to the lead steers, knowing Wash was up front now instead of Colonel Duncan. He noticed the buzzards right away, and he called out to Ron Callahan.

"Trouble ahead!" Jake shouted. "Watch the herd while I have a look."

Jake galloped onward, picking up Wash along the way. Lofland joined them as they topped a hill and gazed down at two deserted freight wagons on the side of the trail.

"Wait here," Lofland urged as he pulled both pistols. He nudged his horse into a trot and approached the wagons with rare caution. Jake couldn't see much beyond the wagons, but when Lofland started back, it was clear somebody was dead there.

"Ride back and fetch a shovel," Lofland shouted to Jake. "Wash, pick yourself out a spot to graze the herd."

"Why?" Wash asked.

"You can't be as big a fool as you sound!" Lofland growled. "We've got trouble here, and it's best the cattle are settled in before we deal with it."

Jake galloped along the herd's left flank until he located the cook wagon.

"Give me the shovel, Josh," Jake called to his brother.

"Josh?" the thirteen-year-old asked. "You never call me that."

"Sorry, Peanut," Jake said, trying to quiet his nerves. "I do need the shovel, though."

"How many?" Doc asked.

"Huh?" Jake responded as Josh passed him the shovel.

"I saw the buzzards," Doc explained. "How many are dead?"

"I don't know," Jake answered. "But by the look Lofland's got on his face, it isn't pretty."

As Jake headed back up the trail, he was filled by a sudden sense of foreboding. He dreaded seeing whatever was on the far side of those freight wagons. More than that, he feared what was sure to follow.

Lofland had mercifully covered the six dead freighters with blankets taken from one of the wagons.

"Don't look," the gunman warned when Jake approached

the closest corpse. The figure beneath that blanket wasn't much bigger than Josh. A smallish hand protruded on the far side. The skin was brownish and swollen.

"They've been here awhile," Jake noted.

"A day at least," Lofland agreed. "Birds got to 'em pretty good. They were a family, I'm guessing. Brothers maybe, along with two of their youngsters."

"Cherokees?" Jake asked.

"Be my guess they were," Lofland agreed. "Must've happened just after Colonel Duncan rode through. He was lucky to've missed out on this."

"I guess," Jake said, plunging the shovel into the sandy earth.

They took turns digging until a single long trench a foot and a half deep had been prepared. Lofland then insisted on dragging the bodies over himself.

"You've seen enough lately to trouble anybody's dreams," Lofland noted.

"Don't you have nightmares, Mr. Lofland?" Jake asked.

"Call me Stan. I'm not so old you need to mister and sir me to death."

"Guess not," Jake admitted. "You didn't answer my question."

"No, I didn't," Lofland confessed. "Let's see. Nightmares? No, I'm past that, Jake. Too many bloody fights to remember half of them."

Jake held his breath as the bodies were placed elbow to elbow. He then hurried to cover them up. They were finished when Jake noticed the buzzards picking at something on a nearby hill.

"There's more of them," Jake said, shuddering.

"No, those are bluejackets," Lofland explained. "They dropped three of 'em. I dragged 'em up that way when you went for the shovel. Leave those varmints to the birds. Hope they choke on 'em."

"What do we do now?" Jake asked.

"Have a look through the wagons," Lofland suggested. "Maybe we can find out who these folks were."

"Didn't they have any papers?" Jake asked. "Pocket books?"

"They were peeled, Jake," Lofland explained. "Stripped bare. I guess those bluejackets were afraid the little boy might have gold dust hidden in his trousers!"

"I'll take the first wagon," Jake offered.

"I got the other one, then," Lofland answered.

Jake began by circling the wagon. There were odds and ends of clothing scattered there, but nothing to identify the owners. Then he climbed up onto the seat and felt around underneath. That was a favorite hiding place of his father's. The thieves had known it, for the wood was splintered as if chopped apart by an ax. Most of the boxes in the wagon bed had been rifled, and the raiders had taken a considerable haul. As Jake lifted a dislodged box of twine, he noticed something below.

"Somebody in here?" Jake called.

He detected a second movement, and he dove at it. Something rock hard clubbed his forehead, and a knee thumped him in the chest and knocked the wind from his lungs.

"Ayyyy!" a smallish figure howled as it tore at Jake's ribs with ironlike claws.

"Stop it!" Jake cried, fending off his attacker with both arms until he could breathe again. He then grabbed the demon by its hair and threw it out the back of the wagon. As he followed in pursuit, he stared with wide eyes at a Cherokee boy a little shy of five feet tall who somehow had gotten hold of his very own Sharps rifle.

"Drop the rifle, boy," Lofland barked, and the youngster turned in that direction. Jake jumped out and tore the rifle from the boy's hands.

"Go ahead!" the Cherokee cried defiantly. "Kill me, too!"

"I haven't killed anybody," Lofland said, laughing. "Not today anyhow. You, Jake?"

"Not even a buzzard," Jake added, coughing. "I might just lay into you a time or two for ambushing me in the wagon, though."

"You aren't with them others?" the boy asked.

"Came up with that outfit yonder," Jake explained, pointing to the dust rising from the herd grazing at the foot of the hill. "These folks your family?"

"Father," the youngster answered. "Two brothers. Cousins."

"What's your name?" Lofland asked. "Where are you from?"

"I'm called Judson Tenkiller," the Cherokee explained. "We live down at Cabin Creek."

"We've been there," Jake said, recalling the place. "They're the ones that warned us about the bluejackets."

"They should know," young Tenkiller muttered. "Enough of us been killed by that bunch."

"No more," Lofland growled. "I aim to put an end to them."

18

"I feel sorry for the boy, too, but I don't see how it's any of our business," Wash argued when Jake and Stan Lofland returned to their companions late that afternoon.

"You don't, do you?" Lofland growled. "You don't know much, then. You can't leave a loaded pistol sitting there aimed at your head. You have to tend to it."

"Those bluejacket fellows are miles away," Wash objected. "You said that yourself."

"We trailed 'em a ways," Jake admitted. "Far enough to see it was safe to ride back here and fill you in."

"Look, Wash," Lofland said, sighing. "Even if we could get the cattle on north without being bothered, those fellows would just sit back here waiting for us to return. Be a better deal for them that way. They'd rather have cash than cattle any day."

"Jake?" Eddie asked.

"I'm no one to hurry and hang somebody," Jake declared. "And I've already had a gullet full of killing. Maybe some of us'll get killed, too. I don't want to bury any friends. Not again. Even so, it seems to me the sort who'd shoot down a small boy and strip off his clothes, looking for Lord knows what, doesn't merit much more living. If Stan says we best go after 'em, I got to agree."

"No point everybody goin'," Eddie grumbled. "How many you figure there are, anyhow?"

"I counted seven horses," Lofland explained. "Two were heavy, like they were carrying goods. That means five riders."

146

"They could have others waitin'," Eddie said, frowning. "How would you go about it?"

"Get the herd on past first," Lofland advised. "Then scout out their camp and lay an ambush. It'd take five good men."

"If somebody can spare a rifle, you got one," Judson Tenkiller volunteered.

"He's a kid!" Wash complained.

"Anybody figure to hold him back?" Lofland asked as he passed the boy a rifle. "I'd go after the man who shot my pa and little brother. I figure he's entitled to come."

"I guess I go, too," Jake said, frowning. "Jer, you look after Jordy and Josh, hear?"

"I got no particular yen to get any older," Len said, grinning.

"Who else?" Lofland asked.

"Eddie and me," Gene said, studying his brother's face. "We know a thing or two about ambushes."

"You're taking the best men," Wash complained.

"Care to step in for one of 'em?" Lofland asked.

Wash turned away, and Lofland spit.

"We leave at first light," Lofland then explained. "Soon as the herd gets moving. Eat up tonight, and rest well. We've got a steep climb waiting for us."

Jake thought it likely. Even so, he sat up after supper, helping Josh scrub the dinner plates. Afterward Jericho and Jordy joined them, and the brothers sat by the fire, recollecting old half-forgotten adventures.

"There'll be other good times, too," Jake vowed when he deemed it time to roll out his blankets.

"Sure," Josh was quick to agree. "Only, Jake, don't take too many chances with those bluejacket fellows."

"It's not that we're extra fond of you, big brother," Jordy added. "It's just none of us has the guts to tell Miz Miranda."

Jake grinned. "Watch your own selves," he urged. "Bluejackets are nothing compared to longhorns."

Jake spread his blankets in his usual place, but Josh

dragged his over alongside, and Jordy added his nearby. Even Jericho and Si made their beds closer than normal.

"We're not expecting trouble tonight," Jake told them.

"We know," Jer replied. "Just seems like we've gotten sort of scattered out lately."

"Yeah," Jake said, nodding. "Doesn't mean you're any of you far away, though."

Jake slept well that night squeezed between his brothers, and he awoke unusually alert. Stan Lofland was pacing behind the wagon. Jake dressed himself hurriedly and joined the gunman.

"Something bothering you, Stan?" Jake whispered.

"No," Lofland said, laughing. "Truth is, I was feeling sort of sorry for myself."

"You?" Jake cried.

"You don't know a whole lot about life, do you, Jacob Wetherby?"

"Sometimes I think I don't," Jake confessed. "Other days I think I've seen and suffered about everything a man can."

"Would it surprise you much to discover I consider you a lucky man?"

"Guess so," Jake said, studying Lofland's eyes. "I never exactly been called that before. A fool. Scoundrel. Idiot. Never lucky."

"I mean because you've got family."

"Got brothers," Jake said, nodding. "A sister back at Harrison's Crossroads. A tiny brother there, too."

"You're close to them."

"Have to be, I guess," Jake said, sighing. "Got no folks anymore. I suppose we rely on each other more than most brothers need to."

"I have a brother," Lofland explained. "If I walked up to his door, he wouldn't open it. He says I carry the smell of death with me. Might be true."

"There's no such thing," Jake insisted.

"No, there is," Lofland argued. "Sometimes a man gets so all he knows is killing and dying. I'd almost welcome death if it came quick and clean. From the front. A man gets himself a certain degree of fame, and people shy away from him. Others step out of shadows, shooting at his back. A man like me doesn't make friends. He does acquire enemies.''

"I judge myself a friend," Jake declared.

"Don't," Lofland urged. "I'm just a man paid to see you youngsters get Colonel Duncan's cows along north.''

"Sure," Jake said, sighing. "Have it your way. But know if it comes to a fight, Jake Wetherby will stand with you.''

"You *are* a fool, Jake.''

"Warned you," Jake said, grinning.

Doc Trimble climbed down from the wagon then and began rousing the others. Jake waited a moment, eager to listen if Lofland had other words to share, but the gunman began packing his gear. Jake left to do likewise.

They didn't speak again for better than two hours. By then the herd was plodding on northward. Jake and Gene Stuart were swinging around the herd to join Lenny Baxter on the left flank. Lofland and little Judson Tenkiller waited for them just ahead.

"It's time," Lofland announced.

"Lead away, then," Eddie urged.

They threaded their way along a narrow trail close to three miles before Lofland halted.

"We're getting closer," he explained. "I'm going ahead. When I wave you on, ride up and stop. We'll take it slow, in little jumps like that. Understand?''

"Sure," Eddie said, nodding.

"I'm going with you," young Tenkiller said, swinging past the others.

"Stay back," Lofland demanded.

"You don't know this country," the Cherokee argued. "I used to hunt with my grandpa around here. There are caves in these hills where a man can hide plenty good. I've got sharp eyes. They won't any of 'em get past me.''

Lofland shrugged his shoulders and waved the youngster along.

Jake couldn't be certain which of them spied the outlaws

first. It was little Judson who rode back with the news, though, and Jake suspected the eagle-eyed youngster was the one.

"Stan says pull your horses off into those trees there," Judson explained, pointing to a tangle of scrub oaks. "Tie 'em good. Then grab your rifles and join us up ahead."

"If I didn't know better, I'd guess we stumbled onto a shrunk-down general," Eddie said, chuckling.

"Might be good to laugh now," Jake observed. "I don't think there's going to be much about what's coming next we'll laugh about."

"Steady, Jake," Gene said, frowning. "Lofland knows his business."

Too well, Jake thought.

When they rejoined Lofland and the Cherokee boy, Jake read something new in the gunman's eyes. They were scary intense. Not nervous. Determined.

"That's them there in the hollow," Lofland explained, pointing to four men dressed in soldier coats, sipping coffee around a cook fire at the base of the hill where Lofland had perched himself.

"The others?" Jake whispered.

"One's watching the other trail," Lofland said, pointing him out. "The other was here."

Jake glanced to his left. A mound of dry oak leaves concealed a body.

"I'll slip over and take the other guard," Lofland explained. "You boys pick out a target around the fire. Wait for my signal. A loud whistle. Shoot quick, but make sure you hit your man. We do it right, it'll be downright easy. Somebody misses, we'll have a scrap on our hands."

"I'll take the bearded fellow on the left," Eddie said as Lofland started toward the guard.

"I got the one by the coffeepot," Gene added.

"Guess I'll take that red-haired fellow," Len said, studying him. "He's skinny, but I guess I can hit him just the same."

"That leaves the youngish fellow there on the right," Eddie said, gazing at Jake.

"No, he's mine," Jake said, creeping forward. He then leveled the Sharps and drew a bead on a sandy-haired fellow in his late teens.

As they readied themselves, Jake knew the others, too, were nervous. An odor of sweat tainted the crisp summer air, and Lenny's feet rustled the leaves.

"Be still," Eddie urged, and Len froze.

Suddenly someone shouted from up the trail. Pistol shots shattered the stillness, and the men at the fire scurried for cover. Eddie hit his man anyway, shooting him neatly just under the chin. He fell like a rock, dead.

Jake managed to get his sights on his man, but the Sharps pulled a hair to the left, and Jake's initial shot shattered the raider's left ankle.

"Missed," Gene grumbled as he fired well wide of his intended victim. Len had patiently held his fire. Now, as his target made a run for the horses, Len shot him flush in the chest.

"Good shot," Eddie remarked as the bluejacket collapsed in a heap.

"Two left at the camp," Gene observed. "Did Lofland get the other guard?"

"I'll take a look," Jake said, crawling past them. He spied Lofland and young Judson Tenkiller twenty feet to the left. At their feet lay the lifeless corpse of the guard.

"Dead?" Eddie called.

"Guard is," Jake replied. "Lofland's fine."

"So what now?" Eddie asked, gazing down at the trapped raiders. They couldn't escape, but on the other hand, they had good cover there. In order to fire at them, a man would have to expose himself.

"Eddie, keep an eye on 'em," Jake said, sighing. "I'll try to get around to the side and root 'em out."

"You'll get yourself shot," Eddie argued. "Stay put and leave that to Lofland."

"He's pinned," Jake noted. "It's up to us."

It generally was, Jake knew.

He crawled through the rocks down the hillside toward the bluejackets' camp, taking care to keep himself low. He was halfway down when Gene started along behind.

"No," Jake said, waving his friend back. Gene only smiled and continued along.

Once Jake reached the foot of the hill, he waited for Gene.

"Two rifles are better'n one," Gene explained. "Now, what do you have in mind?"

"See those trees?" Jake asked, pointing to a line of willows at the edge of the outlaw camp. Gene nodded. "I'll go first," Jake explained. "Come along if you like."

Jake took a deep breath and made a rush for the trees. He got halfway when a rifle barked. Something stung his left foot, but he managed to stumble on to the trees. Once there, he swung the Sharps back toward the camp. When the sandy-haired teen emerged from cover long enough to take aim, Jake fired. His shot shattered the bluejacket's rifle. Eddie fired as well, shattering the fellow's collarbone. Gene killed the man with a clean shot through the left eye.

"I give up!" the last of the thieves cried, waving a white kerchief.

"Keep down, boy!" Lofland shouted as Judson jumped out.

The outlaw pulled a well-concealed pistol and fired. With a single leap driven by some inner fury, Lofland managed to get himself in front of the Cherokee boy and take the outlaw's bullet. As for the bluejacket, he was torn apart by a volley from the hillside. Jake, meanwhile, managed to plug the hole in his foot with a strip of cloth torn from his shirt.

"Are they finished?" Jake called as Gene edged his way into the camp. As Eddie and Len watched, Gene inspected the fallen raiders. One moaned, and Gene grabbed the fellow's pistol and finished him.

"All dead now," Gene announced. "How's the foot, Jake?"

"It's been better," Jake confessed as he hobbled out from the willows. Only now did he see Lofland. The gunman was sprawled out in the rocks ten feet away. A great red stain spread out from a single wound in his chest.

"He saved my life," young Tenkiller mumbled. "Stepped in front of me."

"Lord," Jake said, limping over beside the dying man.

"Maybe . . ." Lofland whispered.

"Maybe what?" Jake asked.

"Maybe . . . my brother . . . will hear. Maybe . . ."

"Sure," Jake said, gripping Lofland's hands. "He'll hear and remember better days."

"You . . . you think so?" Lofland asked. His eyes pleaded for some sort of hope, and Jake was quick to provide it.

"Sure, he will," Jake declared. "It's how brothers are. They never hold the bad parts of a man's character against him. You're always brothers, you see."

Lofland almost managed a smile. Then a fog clouded his eyes and he drifted off.

"No!" Judson shouted, clutching at Lofland's hands. "You were going to come home with me, meet my ma. No!"

"He's dead," Jake said, tapping the boy's shoulder. "He never knew much peace alive. Maybe he'll find some now."

"He earned it," Eddie added.

"Who'd have thought it possible?" Gene asked. "Lofland dead! Shot savin' a kid he hardly knew."

19

Jake sat with Judson Tenkiller while Gene and Eddie searched the outlaw camp. Len located a spade and dug a makeshift trench for the bluejackets. Lofland was tied to his horse.

"I don't want him resting here with those others," Jake had argued, and the others reluctantly went along.

By the time the raiders had been covered up, Gene and Eddie had located two sacks of U.S. mail, a cash box stuffed with bank notes, and a sack of gold and silver coins.

"What do we do with all that anyway?" Lenny asked.

"Split it among us," Gene suggested. "Reward of sorts."

"Some of it ought to go to that boy there," Eddie said, nodding toward Judson.

"There's bound to be some authority around here," Jake declared. "We'll leave it to them to decide."

"And the boy?" Gene asked.

"You've got family at Cabin Creek, don't you?" Jake asked. Judson nodded. "We'll leave him with somebody who can take him home. And if they don't, we'll take him south ourselves when we come back through."

"You figure what we're going to do with Lofland, Jake?" Eddie asked.

"Isn't for me to decide," Jake replied.

"You seem to be settlin' everything else," Eddie noted. "I judged you had somethin' in mind for him, too."

"There's a hill not far from here," Judson told them. "Lots of flowers in the springtime. Be a nice place to rest."

"Bring that spade along, Len," Eddie urged. "Now, we'd

154

best head on hook to the others 'fore Jake there bleeds himself white.''

"I'm hardly even leaking," Jake grumbled.

"Maybe you'd like to run a race or two, then," Gene said, grinning.

"No, I'm willing to get on along," Jake admitted.

By the time they'd covered the half mile to Judson's hillside, Jake's foot had begun to throb. His head was aching, and his vision had begun to blur.

"Leave the boy and me to tend to Lofland," Len suggested when they paused for the burial. "Jake's growin' worse.''

"He's right," Eddie said, gazing over at his brother. "We better hurry him along to Doc.''

The last that Jake remembered of that afternoon was waving a faint farewell to Len and the Cherokee boy. The rest passed in a blur.

Jake emerged from a haze to find himself lying in the back of the cook wagon. His foot was wrapped in strips torn off flour sacks, and Josh was mopping his feverish forehead with a cool rag.

"You waking up, Jake?" Josh whispered.

"Must be, Peanut," Jake mumbled. "I know you're no angel welcoming me to Paradise.''

"You figure you're headed in that direction, Jake?" Josh asked, grinning.

"Not after today," Jake said, frowning. "Not after all this killing.''

"Today?" Josh asked. "You haven't killed anybody today.''

"No? The bluejackets—''

"That was three days back," Josh explained. "You've been out of your head with fever.''

"The Cherokee boy?''

"We left him and the mailbags with a fellow at the Grand River crossing. The money, too. I think Eddie was hoping for a reward, but they didn't offer us even a penny. Wash was pretty mad, saying we should've kept the money. I guess it was your idea to turn it over, huh?''

"Wasn't ours," Jake argued.

"Sure isn't now," Josh said, shaking his head. "They never would've missed a few hundred dollars, Jake. I suppose you're right, though. And we don't need any Cherokee trouble.''

"Doc tended my leg?" Jake asked.

"Cut a hunk of lead out with his fillet knife. You didn't even flinch. When he set that hot brand against the skin, though, you howled like thunder!''

"I don't remember a bit of it, Peanut.''

"You didn't miss out on anything you'd want to do over.''

"I suspect not," Jake agreed.

Josh then offered a cold biscuit, and Jake managed to chew one end of it. His stomach remained unsettled, though, and he rejected an offer of dried beef.

"I've got a carrot set aside for you, too," Josh told him. "Want that?''

"I'll try a taste," Jake said, accepting the carrot. It was left from dinner, but even cold it was soft and easily chewed. Jake found it tasty, and his stomach didn't reject it.

"You rest up now, Jake," Josh said, propping a flour sack full of clothes behind his head. "We're just a day shy of Baxter's cabin now. We'll likely rest up some there.''

Jake closed his eyes and tried to sleep. He did off and on. By evening he regained his appetite, and he insisted on resuming work the following morning.

"You picked the right day to ride," Gene said as he turned right point over to Jake. "I figure that smoke on the horizon's comin' from Baxter's place.''

"Short day, huh?" Jake asked.

"Shortest I can ever recall," Gene answered. "You want to head up and tell Wash? The land hereabouts is planted with corn. We won't make many friends tramplin' a farmer's crops.''

"Sure," Jake agreed, nudging Bailey into a trot. His foot didn't respond well to the jolting, but he swallowing the ache and went on. By the time he reached Wash, a burly fellow dressed in homespun trousers and a cotton shirt was approaching from the opposite direction.

"We're at Baxter's," Jake announced. "That's likely him there."

"Then I guess we'd best turn the herd off to graze," Wash replied.

"Not here," Jake argued. "Somebody's raising themselves a corn crop in these fields. Ask Baxter there. Get him to find us a place."

"Would seem wise," Wash agreed.

Jake spotted two younger men following Baxter toward the herd. Both cradled shotguns. When Wash failed to greet them, Jake waved his hand and called out, "Howdy!"

"Texas?" Baxter replied. "You up from Texas?"

"Born a Tennessean," Jake explained, "but Texas sort of adopted me. Mr. Baxter?"

"The same," the big man answered. "This can't be your herd, son."

"My uncle's." Wash finally spoke. "John Duncan."

"Expected you yesterday," Baxter said, waving his companions away. "Colonel himself'll be along in another day, I'm betting."

"Not that we don't value your hospitality, but I think we'll all be glad to get this drive finished," Wash explained. "Where should we rest the cattle?"

"Best I send one of the boys with you," Baxter said, scratching his ear. "Some of my neighbors aren't as eager to see Texas beeves pass by. Parker! Get atop your horse and show these fellows the back pasture."

The younger of the boys nodded, turned his gun over to his brother, and trotted toward a nearby corral. He wasted no time throwing himself atop a painted stallion. Shortly he was riding out ahead of the herd, waving them along.

Baxter's land lay along Spring River, and the grass there was rich and well watered. The longhorns settled in just fine. Mrs. Baxter, who was a full-blood Shawnee, arrived with a fresh-baked apple pie for supper. Her daughter Josie drove a buckboard filled with baskets of hot bread and pails of milk to the camp.

"Thought we'd make a feast of it," Baxter explained when he arrived later with his three sons. Besides fifteen-year-old Parker, there was an older one, Henry, and a ten-year-old named Billy. The older ones had their mother's dark coloring and high cheekbones. Billy's hair was reddish and his complexion was somewhat lighter. None of the boys held a candle to Josie.

"She's a looker," Jericho declared right off.

She also had a curious nature, and Jer's maimed hand drew her attention. In no time the two of them were walking off toward a nearby spring.

"Your brother there best watch himself," Parker warned Jake.

"Oh, he's not apt to bother her," Jordy insisted. "Jer's on the shy side where gals are concerned. Now Jake here—"

"You don't understand," Parker interrupted. "You may've been on the trail from Texas two months, but the only boys hereabouts for Josie to track are all named Baxter."

Jake grinned. He could just imagine Jer beset by a she-wolf!

As to Baxters, Lenny struck up a conversation about kinship.

"You have any cousins named Joe Ben?" Len asked.

"Nary a one," Baxter replied. "Got a brother by that name, though."

"Shortish kind of fellow with a twice-broke left arm?"

"Broke it once myself," Baxter confessed. "You know him?"

"He was my pa," Len explained. "Till he took sick three years back and died."

"Never heard," Baxter said, sighing. "He ever tell you of his big brother Bull?"

"You him?" Len asked, surprised. "I thought you'd be bigger."

"Was before I had four youngsters to keep pace with. You

got family back in Texas . . . what'd you say your name was?''

"Leonard," Lenny explained. "My friends call me Len or Lenny, though. Got nobody at all now. Hung around with a cousin, but he got himself killed crossin' Red River.''

"Well, you've got family now, Lenny," Mrs. Baxter said, wrapping an arm around her newfound nephew.

"When you finish up here, come on back and stay a bit,'' Baxter suggested. "If you feel the urge to move on, you're free to do so. Won't argue you out of anything. But if you want, we could do with an extra hand.''

"Never much took to farmin'," Lenny explained.

"Pa's been talking about running some cattle," Parker declared. "Would be helpful to have an experienced cowboy around to show us the ropes.''

"Looks like one of us has found himself a family, at least,'' Jordy whispered. "Jake, you think we ought to rescue Jer?''

"He's old enough to be left alone," Jake argued. "Let's go see about getting a slice of that pie.''

Jericho trotted in later, moon-eyed and stumble-footed.

"He looks like a lovesick pup," Jordy observed.

"I'm not lovesick," Jer argued. "Just befriended.''

"Any idea what that means?" Jake asked Jordy.

"Nope," Jordy said, turning toward Jer.

"Don't ask," Jericho warned.

They had other visitors that following morning. A half-dozen horsemen approached from the north, and Wash roused the camp.

"Uncle's John's back," Wash announced.

"That's not the colonel," Eddie said, grabbing a rifle.

"Indians?" Jordy cried, rubbing his eyes.

"Shawnees," Callahan explained, turning to Wash.

"Whoever they are, they don't appear any too friendly,'' Jake observed.

That was an understatement. The Shawnees arrived armed to the teeth and red-faced angry.

"What business do you have bringing these Texas cows onto Shawnee land?" their leader barked.

"They'll spread fever to our stock," a second man complained. "Don't you know that? Do you mean to kill off our animals and starve our children?"

"What are you talking about?" Wash cried. "Look at our cows. Do they appear sick?"

"Oh, Texas cows never catch the fever themselves," the Shawnee leader growled. "Just pass it along to other cows."

"Get off our land!" a slim-faced man on the right shouted. "Go back to Texas!"

"Your land?" a voice boomed out from behind Jake. He turned to see Baxter striding toward the riders. "Just what do you mean, Nathan Otterfoot, riding out and hollering at guests of mine?"

"Should've known," the Shawnee leader grumbled. "You stupid enough to ask 'em here, Baxter?"

"I guess so," Baxter replied. "Seeing as how it's my land, I guess I can be as stupid with it as I care."

"You'll lose all your cows, just like last summer," the thin-faced fellow warned.

"If I do, I can buy new ones with the grazing fees I'm collecting. I suggest you do the same. Other outfits will be coming north."

"We'll stop 'em!" Otterfoot vowed.

"You're outgunned and outthought," Baxter insisted. "You haven't got five or six cows to your name. You could earn fifty dollars a day letting the Texans rest their stock on that acreage of yours near the river. Have it your own way, though. Just leave these fellows be. They're not harming you any."

The Shawnees stared angrily at Baxter and the Texans, but there was nothing they could do. Slowly, reluctantly, Otterfoot turned and rode away. The others followed.

"It's hard for some to see the future," Baxter said, gazing at the swirling dust that marked his neighbors' departure. "We'll all of us make our fortune here on commerce. Texas cattle to Kansas City and Chicago. Freight running south."

"Guess not everyone can see it," Jake noted.

"Hard to, sometimes," Baxter admitted. "They've been

pushed and shoved most of their lives. This just seems like another white man's trick.''

"Sure,'' Jake said, sighing.

It wasn't the last time Jake spoke with Bull Baxter about the future. That same evening, as Doc Trimble turned a side of fresh-butchered beef over the glowing embers of a cook fire, Baxter and Jake gazed at Jericho and Josie walking out toward the sunset.

"Josie says you boys have lost your folks,'' Baxter said. "Like young Lenny.''

"Got a sister in Texas, though,'' Jake explained. "Bitty brother, too.''

"There's a bright future for an enterprising young man in Kansas Territory,'' Baxter explained. "Lots of land to be had cheap. You could put up a house, start with horses and cattle, build up a fine ranch.''

"Thought about doing that back in Texas,'' Jake said, glancing back at Jer. "Might still be wilderness to some, but we Wetherbys are accustomed to the wilds.''

"Might lose more than a finger and some skin off a foot next time, son,'' Baxter noted. "Not so much violence here-abouts.''

"Wasn't all that far away we had it out with those blue-jackets,'' Jake pointed out. "Truth is, trouble can find you anywhere.''

"That's true enough. Jake, my girl's taken a shine to your brother. Be nice to give those two a chance. Jericho could do worse for himself.''

"He's seventeen,'' Jake said, shaking his head. "Lots of time for decisions.''

"You won't consider what I suggested?''

"I'd have to do some deep thinking on it, sir. Speak with my brothers.''

"And if Jericho decided to stay here?''

"Lord, Mr. Baxter, I'm not his pa. Been a long time since he needed me to button his shirt. He'll do what he chooses.''

"I thank you for that at least,'' Baxter said, offering his hand.

20

If John Duncan hadn't returned that next morning, Jericho might have chosen differently. The colonel did arrive, though, and all four Wetherbys rolled their blankets and prepared to continue the drive.

"I've sold the herd, boys," Duncan had told them earlier. "We deliver our cattle to Matt Howard at Fort Scott."

"Where's that?" Jake had asked.

"Sixty miles or so north," the colonel had explained. "We should be there in less than a week."

"We sellin' our stock to the army, then?" Gene had wondered.

"No, Howard's a buyer out of Kansas City," Duncan had replied. "The place isn't a regular army fort now. Just a small town of sorts. Lots of land there for holding cattle. Howard's got men there to tend cattle and others to haul them to Kansas City a hundred or so at a time."

The cowboys had listened attentively, but Jake suspected he hadn't been the only one to be glad when Colonel Duncan sent them out to grab their horses.

John Duncan himself was in an unusually buoyant mood. Except for a sad nod when Wash passed on the news of Stan Lofland's death, the colonel appeared downright jubilant.

"Why shouldn't he be?" Gene asked Jake as they goaded the lead steers into motion. "I'll bet they met his price."

"That's good," Jake insisted as he slapped a rope's end against the rump of a reluctant steer. "When we drove that herd in from the Brazos country, Colonel Duncan paid us all a bonus. I could spend a few extra dollars."

"He ought to pay double," Gene complained. "After all, we're not all of us here to collect wages."

Each cowboy reacted differently to those final days on the Shawnee Trail. Ron Callahan boasted he would empty half the whiskey bottles in Kansas. Eddie and Tip tried to convince Gene they should pool their money and buy some land.

"There's plenty of good horses runnin' free out here," Tip argued. "We could make a good livin' workin' them into cow ponies."

Lenny Baxter rode rather quietly. His eyes often drifted southward, and Jake knew the young man was thinking of the promised home with his uncle and cousins. Jericho, too, glanced southward more than once.

"Jer's moonstruck, all right," Jordy told Jake. "Be hard talking him into coming back to Texas with us."

Jordy himself seemed reluctant to hurry the longhorns north.

"I always favored horses, and I still do, but I'd say a longhorn's not too shy of a horse when it comes to grit," Jordy explained. "You can go and get downright attached to the fool critters!"

"Not me," Jake insisted. "I'm tired of chewing dust and sniffing dung."

The trail to Fort Scott was little more than a market road, and it proved difficult to keep the cattle strung out in a narrow column. They had always been prone to straying, and as they passed into the farm country south of Fort Scott, it often kindled bad feelings. More than once an angry farmer shot a steer or fired off his rifle at a cowboy.

"Keep those Texas cows off my land!" one white-bearded grandfather demanded.

"Don't you know your cattle will kill my stock?" a woman cried.

Twelve miles south of Fort Scott real trouble arrived. Twenty shotgun-wielding farmers lined the road ahead. Wash came riding back to the herd, shouting and waving his hands around.

"Calm down," Jake urged. "What's happening?"

"Stop the herd," Wash pleaded. "Leave somebody to watch 'em and send everybody else up to Uncle John."

Jake did so. When he galloped to the head of the herd, he found the colonel patiently sitting atop his horse in front of the farmers. Once Jordy, Len, Gene, and Eddie arrived, the colonel spoke.

"Friends, you're blocking the road," Duncan noted. "I suppose you have something in mind."

"We do," their leader, a tall man of perhaps forty years with a full white beard, declared. "Go back."

"Mister, I've been two months on a dusty road from Texas," Duncan growled. "I don't see any point to stopping. I don't know what grievance you believe you have, but I assure you it won't stand up to a thousand charging long-horns."

"Texans," the bearded farmer muttered. "I knew it. You slave-owning sons of Satan must return from the hell that spawned you. You aren't welcome here in God's country!"

"Slave-owning?" Jordy said, staring at Jake. "We ever own any slaves?"

"We look like rich men?" Jake asked the farmers. "We're a hair tired, true enough, and I suspect after four days without a wash, we smell some, but I don't see where that's much of a reason for us to go shooting at each other."

"Wish Lofland was with us," Len mumbled.

"Go back!" the bearded fellow demanded again.

"We're going on to Fort Scott," Colonel Duncan insisted. "Not you or all the farmers in Kansas can or will stop us."

"We'll fill you and your boys full of holes!" a younger farmer barked.

"And you, in turn, will be run down by my herd," the colonel explained. "My nephew's back there organizing it."

"Sons of Satan!" the bearded one yelled.

"No!" Jake cried as the farmers cocked their shotguns. "Wait!"

"Jacob Henry, stay out of this!" Duncan demanded.

"I can't," Jake said, nudging Bailey ahead. "Look, mister, I know the colonel. He's made a deal with a fellow at

Fort Scott, and he'll get these cows to him even if it means we all have to die. Now what would that prove? That he's as stubborn as you are? You talk like a man who knows his Bible. Doesn't it talk about turning the other cheek? Do you really want to turn your gun on my brother Jordy here? Me? Lenny? Most of us are already orphans, so I guess we're not much loss to anybody, but you all appear to be family men.''

"I've got eleven children," a beanpole of a man on the far left replied. "Brother Brown, you don't mean to get us killed, do you?''

"I ain't shootin' at these youngsters," another farmer said, lowering his shotgun.

"We'll do our best to keep the stock clear o' your land," Jake added, turning to the colonel. "And if you lose stock, maybe Colonel Duncan here can promise to make your losses good.''

"I will," Duncan agreed.

"They've got no slaves, Pa," a younger man told Brown. "Doesn't seem to me like this is the place to start a war. Nor even the ones to fight.''

"He's right, Brother Brown," the beanpole agreed.

"I thought I stood with stouthearted men," Brown muttered as his little army melted away. "But I suppose I must await a better day.''

Brown remained for a few minutes with his two sons, but the rest of the farmers headed for waiting horses or buggies and headed home. Finally the Browns, too, departed.

"Whew," Jordy said, wiping his brow with a kerchief. "I could go a day or so without seeing those fellows again.''

"That's about all we needed," Gene grumbled. "Lunatic farmers with shotguns.''

"Just protecting their stock," Jake argued. "Their land. Truth is, I didn't see anything all that different about 'em.''

"I was wearing overalls myself a while back," Jordy added, managing a nervous grin.

"It's over now," the colonel noted, waving them back to the herd. "And Jacob Henry, you leave me to handle such matters in future.''

"Yes, sir," Jake said, sighing.

"You ask me," Gene said as he followed Jake back to the herd, "was you saved our hides. The fellow Brown, with the white beard, had crazy eyes. I confess I thought he'd shoot us all down and dance on our graves."

"He was strange, all right," Jake agreed. "Summer's a hard time for dry land farmers. Haven't had much rain lately, you know."

"You'd think you were a seed-sproutin' farmer yourself, Jake Wetherby," Gene said in disgust. "Best reform. You've turned cowboy, remember?"

"Sure," Jake said, nudging Bailey into a trot. "Guess it's time I got back to my work, too."

John Duncan rode at the head of the herd as they approached Fort Scott late the following afternoon. The rumbling herd raised a tower of dust, and Matthew Howard soon galloped out to meet them.

"Swing them over to the river, Colonel," Howard instructed. "We'll do the counting there. My boys'll be along in a bit to help."

"We won't run across farmers out there, will we?" Duncan asked.

"Guess you happened across Brother Brown and his boys, huh?" Howard asked. "Almost sent a man out to warn you. He mostly devotes his energies to hanging proslavery settlers, but I suppose he's taken it into his head to keep Texas cattle out of Fort Scott, too."

Jake didn't bother listening to the balance of the conversation. Instead he waved to Gene and began turning the herd north and west toward the nearby banks of the Marmaton River. As the cowboys eased the longhorns toward the inviting banks of the river, the thirsty longhorns surged into the shallows to cool themselves and satisfy their thirst.

It was another hour, after the animals had been counted and turned over to Howard's outfit, that Jake headed upstream to enjoy the river himself. Jordy, Jer, and Si trailed along. The four of them had barely shed their dusty clothes and plunged into the stream when the Stuarts approached.

Doc Trimble drove his wagon up with Josh afterward. The rest of the cowboys straggled in one by one.

Wash and the colonel didn't arrive until later.

"Don't mean to disturb your amusement," Colonel Duncan called, "but I thought you might care to collect your pay."

The stampede that followed was a fair match for any a thousand longhorns could have managed.

"I first of all want to thank you fellows," Duncan said as he drew a sack of gold pieces out of his saddlebags. "We got better than nine hundred forty head to market. Most of 'em were ones we started out with, too," he added, grinning at Eddie. "They all bore the Bar JD brand, anyway."

The cowboys shared a nervous laugh.

"I promised you each a hundred dollars and a horse at trail's end, but I'd be shortchanging you if I didn't share my success—the success you all made possible. You've suffered along the way. We've buried friends. Some of you've grown tall and hard. I'm proud to shake your hands, and if you get south and are crazy enough to want more dust-choked, summer-baked, and winter-frozen labor around the worst-tempered most addle-brained cuss known to man—and I don't mean longhorns—drop by and see Colonel John Duncan."

"A cheer for the colonel!" Jake called, and the cowboys howled toward the sky.

They quickly got dressed and lined up to be paid. The colonel passed each man seven shiny double eagles—a hundred forty dollars—along with a signed bill of sale for one mount.

"You pick out the horses yourselves," he added. "Just scribble the name in. Or, in your case, Callahan, get one of these educated youngsters to write it for you."

"I can write my name, Colonel," Callahan grumbled. He was nevertheless grinning, and the other jests that followed were in fun as well.

"Don't forget Maizy's waiting for you at Fort Washita,"

the colonel told Jake when he passed the money over. "And somebody else's waiting a hair farther south."

"I know you boys have your heart set on buying up Fort Scott," Doc called as they brushed their clothes and combed their hair in preparation for the ride into town. "I talked the colonel out of a steer, though, and I plan on givin' you a final Texas-sized feed here at the river. Do your worst in Fort Scott, but do an old man a favor by joinin' him for dinner afterward."

"Easy to do, Doc," Eddie told the old veteran. "We ain't had any better offers."

"Besides," Si added, "one of them other fellows said all the gals in Fort Scott look like buffalo."

Jake suspected, though, even if the streets had been lined with yellow-haired charmers, the cowboys would have shared that final evening. It was strange, standing there beside the river. There they were, the four Wetherbys, three Stuarts, Ron Callahan, Lenny Baxter, Ty Wells, Si Garrett, Wash, the colonel, and old Doc—the survivors. The ghosts of others seemed to linger in nearby shadows.

"I know," Jer said, gripping Jake's shoulder. "I can almost hear Ollie whining 'Wild Women.' "

Jake passed an hour in the huddle of old military buildings and log cabins that made up Fort Scott. He soaked in a hot tub and was clipped and shaven by a young woman who claimed to have learned the trade in a St. Louis hospital.

"You ever need another bullet cut out, I do that, too," she said when Jake explained the scar on his foot.

Jordy proudly paid for a shave, even though he was painfully short of whiskers. That soured Josh a little on the bathhouse.

"Only got half wages, too," Josh complained.

"All the better reason to look at the bright side of it, Peanut," Jake argued. "Saved yourself a dollar just now, didn't you?"

"I'd pay a dollar to have that gal hanging over me like you boys," Josh grumbled.

"Well, there's a place over past the saloon where—" Jordy began, but Jake quickly hushed him.

"We didn't fare too well at Fort Washita," Jake whispered. "And all things considered, Josh can wait a year or two for that."

They skirted the saloons as well.

"Lofland's dead," Jordy observed. "Be best not to get killed now, with money in our pockets."

"You'll never look prettier for burying," Jer observed.

"I've got other trails to ride first, Jer!" Jordy insisted. "Horses to break and races to run."

"You know, if we put our money together, we'd still have close to four hundred dollars," Jake said, gazing south. "It would be enough to buy our own land, start up a herd of cattle."

"Horses, too," Jordy added.

"Build a future for ourselves," Jake declared.

"I was thinking about passing some time at Baxter's," Jericho explained.

"You can," Jake pointed out.

"No, some other cowboy's probably come through by now," Jer said, sighing. "Besides, I always did figure on asking Amy Anders to the harvest dance. She'd be a better match."

"Gap-toothed and skinny," Jordy snickered.

"I've filled out some this summer," Jer said, swatting Jordy's rump. "She may have, too."

They went on squabbling and trading jests as they returned to the river. Once there, Jake was surprised to find Lenny and the Stuarts already gathered by the cook fire. Ron Callahan happened along at dusk, and soon the whole company was reassembled.

After stuffing themselves with barbecued ribs, boiled potatoes, and fresh greens, they gobbled bowls of Doc Trimble's best peach cobbler. Jericho fetched Ollie's guitar and started up a song, and their voices joined in a remembrance of the long journey up the trail from Texas.

"Let's have a lighter tune," Doc urged afterward, taking

a swig from a jug Callahan had brought out from Fort Scott. "Here's to friends. Some are gone, but nobody's ever forgotten."

Jake laughed as Doc hopped one-footed around the fire.

"We did all right, eh, Jake?" Josh asked as he squeezed in beside Jake's left elbow.

"We did, Peanut," Jake admitted as he gazed at the bright faces illuminated by the dying embers of the cook fire. They had shared so much!

Here are my brothers, he told himself. He shared a blood bond with three, and the deeper, more profound bond forged by fire and ordeal with the others.

"Hurrah for tomorrow!" Si shouted. "And to a safe journey home."

Jake cheered along with the others.